THE WRECKING

CHRISTY BARRITT

COMPLETE BOOK LIST

Squeaky Clean Mysteries:

#14 Cold Case: Clean Sweep

While You Were Sweeping, A Riley Thomas Spinoff

The Sierra Files:
#1 Pounced
#2 Hunted
#3 Pranced
#4 Rattled
#5 Caged (coming soon)

The Gabby St. Claire Diaries (a Tween Mystery series):
The Curtain Call Caper
The Disappearing Dog Dilemma
The Bungled Bike Burglaries

The Worst Detective Ever
#1 Ready to Fumble
#2 Reign of Error
#3 Safety in Blunders
#4 Join the Flub
#5 Blooper Freak
#6 Flaw Abiding Citizen
#7 Gaffe Out Loud (coming soon)
#8 Joke and Dagger (coming soon)

Raven Remington

Relentless 1

Relentless 2 (coming soon)

Holly Anna Paladin Mysteries:

#1 Random Acts of Murder

#2 Random Acts of Deceit

#2.5 Random Acts of Scrooge

#3 Random Acts of Malice

#4 Random Acts of Greed

#5 Random Acts of Fraud

#6 Random Acts of Iniquity (coming soon)

#7 Random Acts of Outrage (coming soon)

Lantern Beach Mysteries

#1 Hidden Currents

#2 Flood Watch

#3 Storm Surge

#4 Dangerous Waters

#5 Perilous Riptide

#6 Deadly Undertow

Lantern Beach Romantic Suspense

Tides of Deception

Shadow of Intrigue (coming soon)

Storm of Doubt (coming soon)

Carolina Moon Series:

Home Before Dark

Gone By Dark

Wait Until Dark

Light the Dark

Taken By Dark

Suburban Sleuth Mysteries:

Death of the Couch Potato's Wife

Cape Thomas Series:

Dubiosity

Disillusioned

Distorted

Standalone Romantic Mystery:

The Good Girl

Suspense:

Imperfect

The Wrecking

Standalone Romantic-Suspense:

Keeping Guard

The Last Target

Race Against Time

Ricochet

Key Witness

Lifeline

High-Stakes Holiday Reunion

Desperate Measures

Hidden Agenda

Mountain Hideaway

Dark Harbor

Shadow of Suspicion

The Baby Assignment

Nonfiction:

Characters in the Kitchen

Changed: True Stories of Finding God through Christian Music (out of print)

The Novel in Me: The Beginner's Guide to Writing and Publishing a Novel (out of print)

CHAPTER 1

SAMANTHA WHITE never knew fear had a sound until now. With her eyes covered, she could only listen.

She'd heard the noise of crystalized snow crunching beneath heavy footsteps, footsteps that brought with them the uncertainty about her future —about whether she would live or die.

She'd listened to the heavy breathing of someone who was nervous and hovering over her as he plotted her next hours in captivity.

If she closed her eyes, she remembered the flinch-inducing creak of an old door opening, the crackle of a fireplace that didn't remind her of warmth but of the devil, and she remembered . . . silence.

Silence was what she heard when her abductor left her all alone.

Then there was no fire. No footsteps. No heavy breathing.

Except maybe her own.

And she could see nothing.

Not because she was blind. But because of the hood that had been pulled down over her head.

When the man had first covered her head, Samantha had tried to manipulate her body by rubbing her upper half against the couch behind her. She lunged forward and tried to catch the fabric between her knees.

All during the silence.

Of course.

But nothing worked.

She wasn't sure which fear was worse—the fear that she would continue to live this nightmare or the fear that she would die.

She'd heard the stories on the news. Heard the town scuttlebutt. Listened to her friends whisper their fears as if children talking about the boogieman. Only they weren't children. And this boogieman was real.

A serial killer had chosen their peaceful, quiet county for his hunting ground. He'd already taken the lives of seven women.

Seven women whose cars had broken down on the side of the road. Seven women who'd been alone in the crevices of these Virginia mountains, a place where cell service was as scarce as the local's piece of mind since this rampage had started sixteen months ago.

Women tried not to go anywhere alone—but at times it couldn't be avoided. And that was when he struck.

The media had dubbed him the Grim Wrecker—though not all the women had wrecked. Samantha's tire had popped on an icy, secluded road. She'd guess her abductor had planned it that way. Perhaps her abductor had followed her—watched her—and he'd planned down to the last detail how he would grab her.

Except she hadn't even been driving her car. No, she'd borrowed her best friend Elise's car since her own vehicle was in the shop. And Samantha hadn't intended on going out alone, but her mom needed an inhaler. So Samantha had driven to the pharmacy. It hadn't been late or far away. But then she'd run into Hank Turner, and he'd talked her ear off. He'd even offered to give her a ride home after they'd wrapped their conversation, but she'd refused.

After all, tragedy happened to other people.

But this time, tragedy had happened to Samantha.

When she'd heard the pop of her tire, she knew she was in trouble. But before she could react, her car

3

had lurched out of control on a patch of black ice. Her head hit the steering wheel. And everything went black.

She'd woken up here, in the cabin. Her hands and feet were bound. The rope holding her hands had been attached to something on the couch—the frame of a sofa bed beneath the cushions maybe.

It had been two days since her nightmare began. Two days with no food or drink.

The man hadn't hurt her, per se. But he'd watched her. Observed her. Even draped a blanket over her.

What was he planning? When would it begin? How would it end?

Her breath caught.

She heard a sound in the distance. Another round of panic seized her.

Tires crunched across gravel. A door slammed. Footsteps stomped on a wooden porch.

He was back.

Not only that, but it was the third day. She'd followed the news enough to know that was the day the Grim Wrecker always killed his victims.

She let out a guttural cry at the thought.

And the sound of fear surrounded her again as death drew closer.

CHAPTER 2

It had been 1,032 days since the sound of hope had first found her.

The sound of voices in the background. Heavy feet. Hands reaching for her. Her mask being pulled from her head, light blinding her eyes, and the image of three hunters leering at her. Stumbling across her. Rescuing her.

Samantha had prayed that with the hope, the fear would disappear. But nearly three years later, that hadn't been the case. Fear always found her, especially in the silence.

Just as she did daily, Samantha opened the front door to her mountain bungalow in Shivering Falls, Virginia, ready to head to work. Ready to do the one thing that made her feel like she could make things right.

Working with victims of abuse for a local nonprofit was a labor of love.

Maybe if Samantha could help someone else, she could somehow help herself. Maybe she could find healing for her own bruised soul. The prospect of life ever returning to normal seemed like a distant dream.

She stared at her front yard a moment. This place was her haven—her own little one-acre refuge in the mountains. The seclusion might bring some people terror, but to her it felt peaceful, especially on calm days when she could hear the trickle of the creek behind her house.

The creek sounded so peaceful with its leaps and bounds and carefree jaunts.

Except for today.

Today, Samantha couldn't hear the creek, which could only mean one thing—that it was frozen.

This day was gray and dreary, which seemed fitting. Samantha had always liked stormy, turbulent days, but lately this kind of weather matched her moods. And, though most people would think these conditions less than ideal, this brisk day was one more day of living with freedom instead of tyranny.

She'd learned to appreciate that fact.

She pulled on her insulated slicker and opened

the storm door, surprised by how sharp the wind was and how frigid the air felt. Forecasters said they might get some snow here in the Shenandoah Mountains of Virginia, even though it was only mid-October. Temperatures had dipped unseasonably low this week.

Though she liked storms, something about snow always made her wary. Made her want to freeze right along with the creek behind her house. Took her back in time.

Her psychologist had told her that the senses had a way of rousing memories and making them feel present instead of past. He'd said smells could sweep a person back in time. And, for Samantha, everything about this weather tried to transport her back to the worst days of her life.

It was the crispness of the air. The clean, icy scent of the threatening precipitation. The way snow looked innocent and playful, even though it could clothe in white a potential killer.

Samantha pulled herself together, tugged her jacket closer, and stepped outside. As she did, she spotted an envelope on the stoop.

Curious, she scooped down and picked it up from the cheery welcome mat—one with flip-flops and a smiley face on it. It screamed summer, and Samantha knew she should get a new one. But this one had always lifted her spirits.

Her throat tightened as she looked at the letter. Nothing was on the front—no name or address or stamp. The envelope itself appeared to be ordinary—sealed with an adhesive strip. Standard size and variety.

It was probably an advertisement from a local looking for landscaping work or a church inviting her out for a revival. This was a strange time of year for either of those things, but people weren't always logical.

Despite her rationale, her fingers trembled as she pulled the seal from the envelope.

A folded white piece of paper was tucked inside. Samantha slipped it out, expecting to simply scan it and toss the letter away before heading to work. Instead, the crudely written words nearly caused her heart to stop.

I want to stop. But I can't fight these urges any more. You're the only one who can help me. Will you? Please help me, Samantha.

. . .

A scream caught in her throat.

It was him, she realized. The man who'd brought her to the brink of death and back had returned. The Grim Wrecker.

And he knew where she lived.

CHAPTER 3

One thousand thirty-two days after her release, the sounds around Samantha held her captive again.

The sound of an agent tapping his foot beneath the wide, glossy table. The subtle tick of the cheap clock on the wall. The urgency stretching tight throughout the room here at the sheriff's office.

She had called Rick Frost, the agent she'd worked with at the FBI after her ordeal. In the weeks following her rescue—or was it a release?—she'd been questioned extensively about her abduction.

A special task force had been formed to evaluate any evidence she offered. Specialists had come from Quantico. With no answers or leads or new victims, they'd eventually lost interest.

But it had been at least a year since she'd talked to

anyone at the agency. The urgency had melted away like a spring thaw on the heel of a harsh winter.

After her call today, Samantha couldn't stomach the thought of driving alone after getting that note. What if the Grim Wrecker had tampered with her car? What if he was plotting to somehow abduct her again?

Yet the thought of staying at her house brought her panic also. He'd been there. He'd contacted her. Nowhere seemed safe.

A crew was at her place, looking for any evidence. Any footprints or trace fibers or fingerprints would be photographed, tagged, or bagged. Another agent took her to the local sheriff's office, where Agent Frost had met her.

Here, there were files spread out. A timeline had been started on a dry erase board. The sheriff as well as a detective had gathered, and they talked for a minute like she wasn't even there.

As she sat in the uncomfortable swivel chair, she pictured the note again, and her stomach churned with unease.

Her gaze drifted back to the crew who'd been assembled. Frost was in his forties and had flaming red hair, pale skin, and piercing eyes—the opposite of the chilly image his name invoked.

The other FBI agent was new. He'd introduced

himself as Agent Daniel Quinn. He was in his thirties and on the taller side, with a head full of light-brown hair, a pleasant oval face, and controlled movements. Beneath his button-up shirt, she could see the defined muscles of someone disciplined and strong.

Agent Quinn's eyes were kinder than Frost's, and he was quieter—more of a listener and observer. Maybe it was part of their whole good cop/bad cop routine. Samantha had given up on trying to guess these things. Guessing took too much energy.

Apparently, he'd been brought in from Quantico, and he was an expert on serial killers. Something of a one-man team who came to lend his expertise to situations like these.

Her mind went back to the note again.

I want to stop. But I can't fight these urges any more. You're the only one who can help me. Will you? Please help me, Samantha.

Her gut clenched. Bile rose in her. Her head swirled. Every time she thought about the words there, she had the same reaction. Time hadn't lessened how receiving that letter made her feel.

"Are you sure you haven't had any contact with him since you were rescued?" Agent Frost turned from his notes and the skeleton of a timeline on the whiteboard and stared at her, his eyes icy cold and beady.

"I'm sure."

"Because if you know who this guy is, it's better you tell us now," he continued.

"I don't know who he is."

"I think you do."

She pushed away her frustration, pushed away her desire to cry. How many times could he ask her that question? They'd done this song and dance too many times before.

"Now that you ask, I've been working with him ever since he abducted me, and we've been planning this day for years. Is that what you want to hear?" She cringed at the anger in her words, but Frost treated her as if she was an accomplice. She was over it.

"I understand you're getting frustrated, Samantha." Quinn jumped in before Frost could add more fuel to the fire, no doubt. "That's not what we want. We're concerned that this guy is going to strike again. Sometimes we have to ask the hard questions."

"I'm concerned for that also." Her voice wavered with emotion, with memories. "That's why I called you when I got the letter. I don't want anyone else to live through what I've lived through. I don't object to hard questions. I do object to your tone, however."

"You know who this person is," Frost said, as if he hadn't heard her—or hadn't cared. "You have some connection with him. You need to think harder."

Her hand slapped the table as her internal fire ignited again. She wouldn't let Frost make her into a victim again. No, she was an overcomer. That was the message she'd tried to bestow upon her clients, and she needed to live it in her own life.

"I have been thinking about it. I've been through therapy. Tried every different technique out there. But I can't remember anything else."

His gaze remained unchanged. "You don't want to remember."

She squeezed her eyes shut and lowered her head, fighting to remain in control. Even though she was no longer chained and bound, sometimes Samantha still felt like a captive.

Because maybe Frost was right. There was one memory that always hovered on the edge of her consciousness. She didn't know what it was, but she feared it could be the missing clue that would help authorities find this guy. Nothing she'd tried had helped retrieve it, leading her to believe that it was just wishful thinking.

Yet she knew it wasn't.

No matter what she did, that repressed memory stayed beneath the surface, like a person trapped under an ice lake. Like she was clawing at a frozen layer, aware of everything happening above her. But unable to scream. Unable to breathe. Unable to yell for help.

Unable to do anything except wait for her death.

Frost seemed to sense the repressed memory and assume it meant she was guilty.

All she'd done was go to the store to get her mom's inhaler. One act had changed everything. And it would always change everything.

Tears pressed her eyes, and she stood. "I came here trying to help, but I can see now that nothing I say will ever convince you that I had nothing to do with this. I need to go."

She didn't have to sit here and let Frost make her feel like a victim again. She rushed from the room. She didn't have a car here but she would call Elise or her boss, Hank. Then she'd go . . . somewhere. She didn't know where. Certainly not her house. Not with the Grim Wrecker knowing where she lived.

But she wouldn't be a victim again . . . neither at the hands of a serial killer or the FBI.

CHAPTER 4

QUINN CAST a scowl at Frost before scooting his chair out. He didn't know Frost very well yet, but this whole conversation had turned his stomach. Quinn didn't have time to talk about the agent's behavior now.

Right now he had to stop Samantha.

He stepped into the hallway and spotted the woman headed toward the reception area of the small sheriff's office. "Ms. White—wait!"

Quinn wasn't sure if she would stop, but she did. Slowly, she turned toward him. Tears glimmered in her eyes—tears that she was obviously trying to hold back.

He observed her as she approached. The woman was beautiful with her olive complexion and long, dark hair. She had an almost exotic look with her heart-shaped face and large eyes. All that beauty hadn't saved her from living through a nightmare. Had it added that depth to her eyes or had that always been there?

"I'm sorry about Frost," he said, keeping his voice soft. "Please excuse him."

She raised her chin, showing a healthy dose of self-respect. "There's no excuse for him. I came here trying to help and inform, and instead I'm being scrutinized and pressured. My survivor's guilt is already tremendous, and that's on a good day."

He shifted, desperately needing to reach her before their best lead slipped out the door. "I want to hear more about this. So while the guys here are discussing their next moves, could we talk?"

She stared at him, her eyes wide and uncertain. She was trying to figure out if she could trust him, and Quinn couldn't blame her. Trust wasn't something that should easily be given out.

Finally, Samantha nodded. "I've already taken the day off work. But I only want to talk to you. Not Frost."

Relief filled him. "I can arrange that. Let me grab my jacket, and I'll meet you right here. Okay?"

Quinn waited, watching her reaction carefully and fearing she might change her mind. Instead, she nodded again. "Okay."

Quinn hurried to the conference room that would serve as their headquarters. Frost still sat there, staring at a notepad.

"Samantha and I are going to talk," he said.

"Good work," Frost muttered. "Get her to trust you."

Reaching out to the woman wasn't a play on Quinn's part. He was doing his job. "Kindness goes a lot further than whatever method you're attempting to use. The way you treated her was uncalled for. She's our link—the only one who can stop this guy."

"Sometimes I don't think she wants to remember." Frost shrugged, as if he didn't care. "I can't put my finger on what it is, but I've always thought there was something that girl wasn't telling us."

Quinn stared at his fellow agent, trying to read between the lines of what he was saying. "You think she's involved?"

Frost shrugged again, leaning back in his seat and drumming his pen on the table. "I can't say that for sure. But why did our unsub let her go, otherwise? It's never made sense. Maybe she made a deal with him. Maybe she's an accomplice. Who knows?"

Fire ignited in Quinn. Of all the reasons he could use, that was what Frost had gone with? "Why did this guy do anything that he did? He's been a mystery ever since he first struck five years ago. You're out of line."

Frost stared, not saying anything until, "Be careful with her."

Quinn shook his head and grabbed his jacket. Thankfully, Samantha was still waiting for him at the end of the hallway. Part of him had wondered if she'd be long gone after that conversation with Frost. Quinn wouldn't blame her.

Samantha was chatting with the receptionist. The two must know each other. It was one of the perks of small-town living. She still seemed subdued—upset but maybe not unreasonable.

"You mind if I drive?" he asked.

"Not at all, especially since I don't have a car."

The weather felt surprisingly brisk outside as they stepped into the parking lot. He'd gotten used to the weather in Texas. He'd liked it there in the Lone Star State, but he was happy to experience the four seasons again since he'd moved to the DC area. Besides, it was closer to home.

"They say we're going to get some snow," he murmured, trying to make small talk. He glanced up at the pregnant gray clouds. Soon, the landscape would be covered in icy precipitation.

Samantha shoved her hands into her pockets as she trudged along beside him. "That's what I heard.

It always makes driving around here tricky. Ice and mountains don't mix well, even for people who grew up around here."

Quinn wondered if there was a hidden meaning to Samantha's words. The Grim Wrecker had always struck when road conditions were poor. Now, just as the weather took a turn for the worst, the serial killer appeared to be gearing up to strike again.

The thought made his stomach churn. He'd been studying the man for years, but he'd hoped the guy wouldn't strike again. Every life lost was one too many.

"You from this area?" he asked.

He'd read Samantha's file before, but he needed to find some common ground and establish rapport with her. It wasn't to get on her good side as Frost might assume; it was just common decency. It was about caring for people for who they were and realizing that every person was valuable.

Samantha drew up her shoulders, as if trying to keep the wind from around her neck. "I am. Grew up in this county."

"Have family here still?"

A quick frown pulled at her lips, then disappeared as quickly as the snowflakes dissolving in the air. "Dad died of cancer when I was six. Mom got remarried two years ago and moved to Georgia. No brothers or sisters."

Yet she was still here. Twenty-five years old. Active in the community. Voted Most Friendly in high school.

He'd seen her pictures from back then. She looked so carefree and happy. A different guy had been by her side in all the old photos from her yearbooks. No doubt they were all admirers.

Yet she'd never married.

Was that because she hadn't found the right person? Or had the Grim Wrecker ruined her? Because, on the surface, Samantha seemed like marriage material. Not only was she beautiful, but she seemed kind and strong.

It would seem like such an awkward question to pose to her, but he was curious. The more he knew about her, the easier it would be to put together a profile. He wouldn't ask the question yet, though.

"You ever tempted to leave?" he asked instead. "Start over some place new?"

The snowflake frown made another brief appearance before melting. "Tempted? Always. But this is home, and I don't want some crazy man to drive me away."

"I can respect that."

She stole a glance at him, her intelligent eyes

studying him. "How about you? Where are you from?"

"I just got transferred to DC from Houston."

"Are you having some culture shock? Shivering Falls isn't quite Houston—although, I assume you usually work out of the DC office."

He smiled—almost. "No, I can't say I'm having any culture shock. Both places have their charms, so I can't complain."

"DC has charms?"

He did smile this time. "In its own way."

When they reached his FBI sedan, Quinn opened her door and waited for Samantha to climb inside. Then he got in behind the wheel. As soon as he cranked the engine, he turned on the heat. Cool air blew from the vents.

"Just a few minutes, and it will warm up." He held his hand in front of the vent on the dashboard.

"I'm used to the cold." She stared out the window.

As if nature had heard her, a snowflake hit the windshield. If it was already snowing in October then they were in for a long road.

He waited just a moment longer for the car to heat up before pulling out. "Know anywhere to grab some coffee? This isn't my turf."

She nodded. "Java Hut isn't far away."

Five minutes later, they pulled up to the coffee-house. Java Hut was nestled into a string of shops on a quaint downtown street of Shivering Falls. Nothing about the area screamed that this would be the breeding ground of a serial killer. No, everything about it seemed too down-home and safe—which only made these crimes somehow more horrific.

The scent of cinnamon and vanilla greeted them when they walked inside, aromas that were sure to calm—however so slightly—any nerves. Quinn and Samantha sat across from each other with coffee in hand at a corner table, away from any listening ears.

This was his style. Conversation. Talking. Making people comfortable. He knew how to use his brute strength when necessary, but he preferred other methods.

Maybe he understood it better than the average FBI agent since he'd been a victim at one time also. His parents had been killed in a home invasion when he was seventeen. Their killer was now behind bars for life, but Quinn remembered what those days were like. They'd been bleak, to say the least.

Quinn mentally reviewed what he knew about the serial killer.

Seven victims, all lured into the killer's trap after their vehicles had broken down on lonely mountain roads. Seven bodies found buried in shallow graves at small private cemeteries—left there like they belonged. Seven families who'd grieved without answers.

Only one person had survived. Samantha White.

The killer had tased her and then dumped her on the side of the road. By the grace of God, hunters had found her in the otherwise hardly traveled area.

She was the FBI's best lead in finding out who was behind this.

"Do you ever just stop and listen to the sound of coffee being poured?" she asked.

Her question caught him off guard. "I can't say I do."

"It's really a marvelous sound. So is the sound of rain hitting the roof or a fish tank bubbling or children laughing."

He waited for her to continue.

"You learn to appreciate those things when they're taken away from you," she concluded. "But it's the small, simple things that can bring the most joy."

"It makes sense." He stared at the woman across from him as she sat there stiffly, still probably in shock. "I thought you might be more comfortable talking here."

"Anywhere absent of Agent Frost works for me." She frowned.

Quinn shifted, wondering what their story was. Frost certainly hadn't shared. "He doesn't have much tact."

"To say the least."

"Did something happen between you two?" Frost was married, so it wasn't any type of romantic conflict. At least, Quinn hoped it wasn't.

A shadow crossed her face. "He's never liked me, but his hostility seems to be growing. I assumed he was like that with everyone."

"I've only worked with him one other time, so I can't confirm or deny that." But he was curious about the shadow. She knew more—or suspected more, at least—than she was letting on.

He bit back what he wanted to say—the questions he wanted to ask. They did need to stay focused right now. "Of course. We need to figure out who's behind this."

"I don't want anyone else to go through what I did. It wasn't just my friend's car that wrecked that night. My life has been wrecked afterward. Every day I keep trying to pick up the pieces."

"You seem to be doing a fine job with that."

"Sometimes I just don't know. So I keep moving forward."

"That's half the battle." He shifted. "Look, I know you've been over this a million times. But never with me. I'd like to hear from your own mouth what happened to you, Samantha."

She stared into her coffee and didn't say anything for a minute. Her lips twitched as if she was trying to form the words while battling emotions at the same time.

Before she could speak, Quinn's phone buzzed. He saw it was the office and took the call. The color drained from his face as another agent gave him an update.

"What's wrong?" Samantha asked as he lowered his phone.

"A woman was reported missing this morning. Police just found her car."

CHAPTER 5

I DON'T WANT to do it. But I can't stop myself.

And now here I am. Another woman pleading for her life is bound in front of me.

And I have these urges that I can't contain.

Sweat covers my forehead, and my heart races with anticipation. With urgency. With a touch of hesitation.

There's only one person who can help me. Only one person who helped me overcome before. I tried reaching out. But I was too late.

I glance at the woman. At her thin figure. Her fair skin. At the way her body is hunched over into a ball.

As if that will help her.

These women need to pay. Need to suffer for what they've done to me.

But not Samantha. She has no reason to suffer. She's pure and lovely and kind.

Her picture flutters through my mind, bringing a smile to my face. Making me wish she was here instead of this woman.

Samantha makes me stronger. She always has been special to me—not someone I could ever hurt.

The woman whimpers again and pulls her knees closer to her as she huddles on the couch.

Mandy is her name.

I know all about her. Know her schedule. Her habits. Her friends.

I spent weeks observing and watching, yet never being seen. Blending in.

Then she rejected me, just like the others. Women who think they can carelessly toss me aside, like I don't matter. Women who think I don't make enough money, even though I'm doing a valuable work. That I'm not handsome enough to be by their side. Who don't understand my personality.

They deserve to pay for their quick judgments. For the fact that they don't care if they hurt me. They need to know rejection also. The ultimate rejection —death.

I glance at my watch—a cheap one I bought at a drugstore. The numbers there stare back at me.

It's time to get to work. At my real job. The one

where no one knows I'm a killer. No one suspects me. In fact, they all like me and say I'm a decent guy whose been dealt a bad hand.

I'll have to finish this later.

I look at Mandy one more time. Listen to her cry. Whimper. Beg for her life.

Her time is coming to an end. As soon as I return, I'll finish what I started. I'm not wasting any time this round.

CHAPTER 6

SAMANTHA'S HEAD began to spin at Agent Quinn's words. Another woman missing? Her car found?

Already?

But Samantha had just gotten the note this morning. She hadn't had time to do anything to stop this guy, to heed his cry for help. She'd thought she'd at least have a few days to figure out a plan. Why had he bothered to ask for help, to give Samantha hope that maybe she could stop him?

But apparently the Grim Wrecker had sent the note right before starting his deadly rampage again. He'd never really wanted Samantha's help at all. No, maybe he'd just wanted to play with her head—or announce he was back. Then again, maybe it was all a game to him.

"Was there . . ." She paused, hardly able to say the words. "Was there a key left?"

He nodded, his jaw flexing. "There was."

That was the Grim Wrecker's signature. He always left a car key with no teeth in it—something generic that linked all the crimes back to him. It was his calling card, of sorts.

"I need to get to the scene." Quinn's words pulled her back to the present. "I'll take you home, and maybe we can finish this conversation later."

"Can I go with you?" She hadn't meant for the words to leave her lips, but she didn't want to take them back either.

There had been no victims after Samantha had been released. Not until today. But maybe being at the scene would help her break through that ice barrier her mind had created.

Agent Quinn stared at her, studying her with his intense brown eyes. "I'm not sure that's a great idea."

"Maybe something will be triggered." Her voice caught as she realized the reality of those words. She could be opening a floodgate. But the emotional distress she might endure would be worth it. "I want to help. I really do."

Finally Quinn looked away and offered a curt nod. "I'll need to have you cleared first."

"Of course." She pulled her coat closer as she

followed him outside. The chill wasn't from the frigid weather—this chill had started inside her.

This couldn't be happening again. It just couldn't. Terror had gripped this community three years ago, and people were just now beginning to recover.

Quinn talked on the phone to someone as they hurried to his car. His gaze wandered around them, as if he was searching for the killer. Maybe he was.

A shiver crawled up Samantha's spine, a quake that turned into a quiver that wouldn't recede.

As before, Agent Quinn tucked her into the car before climbing in himself. He hung up and turned to her, his face grim and serious. "You've been cleared; you can come with me. You're right. Maybe it will help you remember."

"I can only hope."

He stared at her another minute, still not starting the car. "But I've got to warn you, Samantha, that this could set off some PTSD. I need you to know what you're getting into."

The fist in her stomach squeezed tighter. "I know. But . . . I'm prepared to live with that."

Samantha said little as he pulled away from the familiar streets of downtown and sped toward the country roads beyond it. Try as she might, she really couldn't prepare herself for this.

She'd secretly hoped the killer had died. Maybe

that was why he hadn't struck in so many years. Maybe something had physically stopped him— maybe God had stopped him through cancer or a car accident. What else would explain his absence?

Or maybe that had all been wishful thinking. Maybe the man had been out there lurking all these years, trying to resist his impulses but unable to. What had set him off now?

She stared out the window. A light layer of snow tinged everything in white—much like the day she'd been abducted. Only there'd been black ice also.

They traveled into the heart of the mountains. The road was just as lonesome as she'd imagined it would be. The narrow stretch was steep, surrounded by woods and jagged cliffs. There was barely a shoulder. And there wasn't a house in sight.

Finally, Agent Quinn pulled up behind several other sedans and police cruisers.

Samantha's heart pounded in her ears. This felt surreal, like a nightmare she'd wake up from. But this was really happening. Again.

Quinn kept a hand on her elbow as they walked toward the police cars. He flashed his badge, and they ducked under the police line. Frost waited in the distance, talking to a local officer.

The entire road had been closed. But she saw the blue sedan in the distance, and she instinctively knew it belonged to the victim. Her heart squeezed again as she imagined what the woman might be going through.

Waking up. In a shack. Bound. Unable to see. Feeling overwhelming fear that squeezed her throat until she felt lightheaded.

Had the woman had any clue as to what was happening when she pulled off on the road's shoulder? Maybe if she'd been in the area three years ago. But someone new to this place wouldn't necessarily know. Wouldn't have felt that familiar fear that the headlines had induced. No one in the area had felt safe for years now.

No one had wanted to ride in their cars alone or at night or on lonely roads. Car pools had been set up. Guns had been purchased.

Samantha had bought a gun, but it had done no good.

She'd hit her head when she wrecked, and didn't remember anything until the time she woke up in the strange cabin.

Samantha's stomach clenched again as they approached Frost. His eyes narrowed when he saw her, but he said nothing. And that was probably only because Quinn was with her. Frost was on his best behavior for the time being.

A steady smatter of icy snow continued to fall

around them. The weather seemed to match her mood—chilled, bleak, promising hardship. The wind blew away any hope of safety or peace. The slick road hinted of danger, that one move could end in injury—or worse.

"What do you know?" Quinn said, bristling with every step closer to Frost.

Samantha could sense it. Quinn didn't like the man either. He scored major points for that.

Frost looked at his notepad. "Our victim left work at the hospital last night around midnight. She's single and lives about three miles from here. It looks like someone messed with her muffler. From all appearances, she pulled over when she began having car problems. She was supposed to meet a friend for lunch and never showed. A trooper came across this vehicle only an hour ago."

Samantha fought to remain in control. Everything inside her wanted to fall apart. To be swept back in time. Her heart hammered in her ears.

This nightmare couldn't be starting again.

"Name?" Quinn asked.

Frost looked at his notepad again. "Mandy Morrison."

Samantha gasped, and both men turned toward her.

"I know her," she whispered, the woman's image filling her thoughts. "I know Mandy Morrison."

Quinn took one look at Samantha's pallor and grabbed her elbow before she passed out. She wobbled but steadied herself.

He exchanged a look with Frost at Samantha's revelation. Quinn hadn't expected the connections to come so quickly, so easily. Yet there it was, begging for attention.

"How do you know Mandy?" Quinn asked once some of the dazed look faded from her eyes.

Samantha squeezed the skin between her eyes, her breathing still labored. But she finally drew in a shaky breath and raised her head. "I worked with her as a victim advocate. She was in an abusive marriage, and she left her husband. I was helping her through the process."

Helping others seemed like a respectable career and life choice for Samantha, Quinn thought. Better than getting buried in fear and paranoia. Wasn't that the same reason he'd become an FBI agent? To somehow find justice in a world that had been so unjust to him?

Frost frowned and his aloof gaze seemed to sear into Samantha. "What else do you know about her?"

Samantha drew in another shaky breath and released it in an icy puff. "She moved here from Pennsylvania around two years ago. She doesn't have kids. She's recently divorced, likes to white-water raft, and . . . I don't know what else to say. She's a really sweet woman."

"When did you meet with her last?" Quinn asked.

"Two days ago." She swallowed hard. "She didn't share anything new. In fact, she seemed happy and ready to move on. She'd even gone on a couple of dates since her divorce has been finalized."

Quinn shifted, processing this new information. "You didn't know any of the other victims, did you?"

"I knew two," Samantha said. "They weren't friends or anything. But this is a small town. One woman, Sarah Storm, went to high school with me. She was a couple of years older. Another woman, Trixie Smith, worked with me at the law firm when I first started there."

"Law firm?" Quinn tried to recall the notes he'd read on Samantha. He didn't remember that.

Samantha nodded. "I was a paralegal before . . ."

She didn't need to finish.

"That's right." Quinn turned toward the road. "We can safely assume that he didn't take his victim through the woods. He used a stun gun on most of them and most likely put them in his trunk—based on the tire tracks at other scenes. Then he took them to a location we've never been able to pinpoint."

She shivered. "All I remember is that it seemed like a shack in the middle of nowhere. I couldn't hear traffic or neighbors or even a creek. Just quiet."

"Nothing about it seemed familiar?" That familiar edge of skepticism in Frost's voice.

Samantha visibly bristled. "No, nothing."

"No evidence of other women being kept there?" he continued.

She shook her head back and forth more adamantly. "Not that I could tell, but I had a sack over my head—in case you haven't read my file or asked me this a million times already."

Quinn gave the man a warning glance. If this behavior continued, he would report Frost. It was uncalled for.

He'd have to think about that later. Right now, they had other matters to attend to.

"We need to track down Mandy's ex-husband— he should be the first person we look at," Quinn said.

"Not the serial killer?" Samantha blinked in confusion.

"Her ex could have staged things to make this look like the Grim Wrecker," Quinn said. "We always look at spouses first, as a general rule. We need to put together a timeline for Mandy and figure out who saw her last."

"I'll look into her ex-husband," Frost said, pulling out his phone as he walked away.

"I'll start on the timeline," another agent said.

At that moment, Samantha's cell rang. A wrinkle formed between her eyes as she stepped away and put the device to her ear.

When her face paled, Quinn knew something was wrong.

Again.

CHAPTER 7

IT WAS him on the other line. The Grim Wrecker.

Samantha was certain of it.

Even though there were no words coming through the speaker, only heavy breathing, her gut told her the killer had called her. Had reached out. Again.

Quinn rushed toward her and put his ear next to hers. The scent of his piney cologne brought her a brief moment of comfort and strength.

This was a pivotal moment. Deep in her bones, Samantha could feel it as surely as she felt the sharp wind through her jacket.

"Who is this?" she asked softly, her gaze fixated on the woods.

The person on the other end just breathed. Heavy. Long. Wordless.

Dear Lord, I need Your guidance now. Please. I beg You.

"It's you, isn't it? The man who . . ." She considered her words, trying to choose them carefully. She licked her lips, which suddenly felt chapped and unbearably dry. "You're the man who let me go."

The breathing stopped for a minute until all she heard was the buzz in her ears.

"Thank you for doing that," she continued, praying she was doing the right thing. A whole team of agents had gathered around her to listen, but she ignored them. "For letting me go. You can do it again, you know. This doesn't have to end like the others did. You can let Mandy go."

The heavy breathing starting again, the sound sending another round of shivers up and down her spine. She recognized the sound. Remembered it. If she closed her eyes, she went back there again. On the couch. Feeling the man's presence nearby. Feeling him as he watched her. Hearing him breathe.

Quinn nodded beside her, motioning for her to keep the conversation going.

"You can turn this around." She knew she had to use every moment while she had his attention. She couldn't squander this opportunity. But the pressure between her shoulders felt like a boulder of ice had been placed there. "Your impulses don't control you. You make the decisions about everything you do."

The breathing continued, faster now, as if he was getting anxious.

"Let her go." Samantha's voice was pleading and soft. She had to reach him. She had to. "Please."

The inhalations came even faster.

Then she heard a click.

The line went dead.

And, as reality hit her, everything spun around her in a blur of white.

Quinn swooped forward and caught Samantha's limp body before she hit the asphalt. He lowered her onto the barricaded road and gently slipped his arms from beneath her lithe figure.

"Someone get her some water," he ordered. "And get a trace on that number."

Quinn doubted they'd be able to track down the location of the caller, but he had to at least try. They had to pursue every lead possible. This guy had to be stopped before he harmed anyone else.

An agent grabbed Samantha's phone and hurried off.

"We need a paramedic over here," he called.

He looked down at Samantha's picture-perfect face—even with her slack, unaware features. His heart went out to her. Maybe bringing Samantha here wasn't a good idea. He wanted to protect her, but he wasn't sure he could.

One of the paramedics rushed over from a nearby ambulance and placed a hand on her forehead to stabilize her. Frost and another agent, Marks, rushed over also.

"It's Samantha," the paramedic muttered. "I didn't know she was here."

"You know her?" Quinn asked, glancing at the twenty-something man with dark hair as he lowered his head toward hers, listening for her breathing.

"We went to high school together," he said. "I'm Aaron. She's still breathing normally and her pulse is strong."

"It must have been the shock of all this," Quinn said. "I caught her before she hit the ground, so the fall shouldn't have injured her."

Just then, Samantha's eyes fluttered open.

"What . . .?" She pushed herself up on the palms of her hands and raked a hand through her thick hair, her eyes narrowed with confusion.

"You just passed out," Aaron said. "You should

lie down. We'll get you a blanket and some oxygen. How do you feel?"

"I'm . . . I'm fine. Don't waste your resources on me. Please." She turned back to Quinn. "Were you able to trace the caller?"

Quinn shook his head. "No, not yet. It's a long shot, but someone is working on it."

He helped her to her feet, and she stood there in silence for a minute, as if getting her balance.

Aaron nodded at him and stepped back, indicating that she should be okay. Quinn appreciated that the man was giving them a moment of privacy. Every minute mattered right now.

"He called." Samantha's eyes, full of depths of fear and exhaustion, met his. She'd probably thought it was a nightmare and felt a jolt when she realized it wasn't.

"I know. You did a good job speaking with him."

She rubbed her forehead, her gaze still a jumbled mass of emotions. Propping her hip against his sedan, she drew in a deep breath. "I didn't know what to do—if I should yell at him or try to appeal to him."

"I think you made a wise choice."

Her uncertainty was evident in her gaze. "I want to help you find him."

As Samantha's words hit his ears, everything in Quinn rebelled. He'd seen the effect of stress on her, and he didn't want to put her through this any more than necessary. This was a lot for anyone to handle. "I'm not sure you're ready for that."

Fire lit in her gaze. "I can be. This is the second time this psycho has reached out to me. If he does it again . . ."

"Maybe we can track him down," he finished.

She nodded. "Exactly."

He rubbed his jaw, the moisture from a snowflake melting on his skin. Having her along would only make things more complicated. But Samantha could also add a lot more insight to this than the average person.

"Let me talk to my boss back in DC," he finally said. "Until then, I need to take you somewhere to rest."

"But—"

He cut her off. "You can't help without approval, Samantha. And I think you need to rest for a while. Is there someone you can stay with?"

She frowned but didn't argue. "My friend Elise."

"I can take you there. We're going to station one of our agents outside the home, just to be safe."

She nodded again. "Okay."

He paused and gripped her arm, wishing he could tell her everything would be okay. But he couldn't make that assurance. Instead, he said, "Samantha, we're going to get through this."

And one way or another, they would.

CHAPTER 8

JUST AS PROMISED, Quinn escorted Samantha to Elise's house. It was located only fifteen minutes away, in an older subdivision full of small bungalows.

Samantha's head spun on the drive there as she remembered everything, as memories rushed back. As threats of yesterday pulled at the present.

"Do you mind if I check things out first?" he asked once they were inside.

"Of course not." She glanced at her friend. "Elise?"

Her friend shrugged. "Go right ahead."

Samantha watched as he went from room to room. As he checked each window and door. Finally, he returned to them at the entryway where they'd huddled.

"Everything is clear," he said. "But here's my

card. Program my number on your cell phone, just in case you need me for anything."

"I will."

Quinn stared at her another moment before finally saying, "Otherwise, I'll check in with you tomorrow."

She didn't want him to leave. She felt better when he was around. But she knew he had work to do and that he couldn't dedicate his time to keeping her safe.

As soon as he was gone and the door was closed, Elise pulled her into a hug.

"I'm so sorry, Samantha," she muttered. "I can't believe this."

Samantha nodded almost stoically. The truth of this still hadn't quite hit her. As she pulled away from her friend's embrace, she drew in a deep breath. Her friend's cute little bungalow had always been comforting.

There was something about the familiar scent of apples and honey that soothed her. Flames danced from a couple of nearby candles. The burn on the wick there was small and simple enough to be comforting—unlike that in a fireplace might be. Her revulsion toward fires was a remnant of her time in captivity, she supposed.

Elise and Samantha had been friends since elementary school when they'd been assigned to sit next to each other in Mrs. Pendleton's class. They'd been inseparable since then. Today, Elise worked as a dental hygienist. She was divorced—her marriage had only lasted six months, and she'd vowed to remain single for the rest of her life. It had given the two friends a lot of bonding time.

Samantha sat on a wingback chair—more like collapsed there—still reeling from today's events. "I can't believe all of this has started again either. Have people heard?"

Elise nodded grimly. "Everyone is talking about it. I've already had five phone calls from people warning me not to go anywhere alone."

That wasn't necessarily a bad thing. People should be cautious. Maybe prudence could save a life.

"I knew her." Samantha's throat tightened as she said the words.

Elise gasped. "What?"

"It's true. I've worked with her through my job at the nonprofit."

Elise sank into the chair across from her and pulled her knees to her chest. "Samantha, that can't be a coincidence."

"It has to be a coincidence," Samantha muttered. "I didn't know all the other victims."

"But . . ."

Samantha knew what Elise was about to say. "I know. He seems to like me. I don't know why. I . . . I just don't know anything right now. Nothing makes sense."

"It was supposed to be me." Elise's shoulders slumped—not dramatically, necessarily. It was with obvious burden and years' worth of guilt.

"Don't say that."

"You know it's true. That . . . that man. He plans his actions. He was supposed to grab me." She covered her mouth to muffle a cry. They'd had this conversation before. Both dealt with a variety of survivor's guilt.

Samantha closed her eyes. Her friend told the truth. From a distance, Samantha and Elise looked similar. They both had dark hair and an olive complexion. As teens, they'd told strangers who struck up a conversation that they were sisters, and some had believed them. Back then, they'd also worn their hair in a similar fashion. Now Elise's was short and bobbed while Samantha's was long and wavy.

"If this is all linked to me, I don't know that I could live with myself," Samantha said.

Elise squeezed her shoulder. "Oh, honey. Everyone knows you have the biggest heart of them all. You're the person who insisted on making muffins for all the elderly at our church."

"Then I got home and tasted one. They were terrible."

"And you were friends with Jed when no one else would talk to him in high school."

"I hate bullies, and he had such a rough life."

"And you're always the first to show up when something bad happens in a person's life." Her tone turned serious. "There's a lot to be said for that. I'm pretty sure everyone cheered when you walked into our high school reunion last month."

"That was your imagination."

"Aaron cheered."

Samantha paused. "What?"

"Aaron Jeffries."

"What are you saying?"

"Oh, come on. Everyone knows he's had a crush on you for years."

"No, he hasn't." Samantha would have known. "But he was at the scene today. As a paramedic."

"Small world," Elise said.

Samantha's phone rang, and she recognized the number. "Excuse me a minute. I need to take this."

Samantha slipped into a spare bedroom to take the call. "Hey, Hank."

"Samantha? Are you okay?" he rushed, the concern evident in his voice.

"I'm fine." She lowered herself onto the bed, suddenly feeling the exhaustion of the evening. As the darkness crept up behind her, Samantha's heart raced. She quickly flipped on a light.

No, no one was there. She was just paranoid.

"I heard what happened. What can I do? Do you need a place to stay?"

Her boss was always both considerate and attentive. She appreciated those qualities about him. "No, I'm with Elise. I'll be fine."

"I love Elise, but she's not going to be much protection if this guy shows up."

"There's an FBI agent stationed outside," she tried to assure him.

"An FBI agent?" His voice trailed off. "That sounds serious."

"It *is* serious, Hank."

"Do they think this guy is coming after you?" His voice turned even more grim.

His words caused Samantha's stomach to churn. "I'm not sure. They're just not going to take any chances until they know what's going on."

He paused. "I can't believe this . . ."

"No one can." It still seemed surreal to her, like a

bad dream she'd wake up from—only the nightmare kept drawing her back in and she couldn't escape.

Hank was someone else who felt guilty. He should have insisted on giving her a ride home. That's what he always told her.

Samantha suspected he liked her. When she'd decided to change careers, Hank had been the first person she'd gone to. But she only felt friendship toward the man—no sparks or visions of forever.

Besides, dating wasn't at the top of Samantha's priority list. Who'd want to be with someone as neurotic as she felt? She couldn't sleep at night. She had nightmares. She wouldn't drive alone at night.

It was a lot of baggage to bring into a relationship.

Hank was a kind and sweet man who ran a nonprofit, going without pay sometimes. He'd started the shelter in memory of his mom, who'd been in an abusive marriage herself. The work he did was honorable and worthwhile.

"I'm scared for you, Samantha," he finally said.

She didn't bother to hide the truth. "I'm scared too."

CHAPTER 9

SAMANTHA HADN'T SLEPT all night. Now it was 5:30 a.m., and she was up, drinking some coffee at the cozy kitchen table. Papers were spread in front of her as she tried to sort out her thoughts.

By now, the police should have talked to Mandy Morrison's family, Samantha realized. She should call them herself, but she couldn't bring herself to do that yet. She was too shaken right now and would probably only add to their stress.

They were grieving, no doubt. Perhaps there was a touch of hope that Mandy would be found alive. Like Samantha had been found alive.

Samantha wanted to hold onto some hope also. The killer *had* called her. Maybe that meant he was second-guessing all of this.

Had her words had any impact on him? Could she even hope?

She sighed and stared at her jumble of notes. Samantha wasn't a detective. She had no desire to be a detective. But what was the connection between all these victims?

She stared at the list she'd started.

Victim #1: Earnestine Fletcher. Schoolteacher. Everyone thought her car had simply broken down, and she'd disappeared. She'd always been flighty.

Victim #2: Riley Durham. Cashier at a gas station. When she'd disappeared in the same manner as Earnestine and the same generic car key had been found, people became more suspicious.

Victim #3: Kelly Levering. Babysitter. When she disappeared, the FBI was called in and things got real. No one could deny the pattern that had emerged. A week later, all their bodies had been discovered.

There was also Sarah Storm who'd gone to high school with Samantha and Trixie Smith, whom Samantha had worked with. Another woman was a horse trainer. Another was attending college.

Samantha stared at the list and frowned. None of the careers matched. Some women were single; some married. Some wealthy; some poor. Some thin; some overweight.

The only connection was that the women were all under thirty. If her notes were correct, the oldest had been twenty-seven and the youngest nineteen. A few of these women had lived in town, but several had lived on the outskirts. One had been visiting from another state. Though Samantha's little town was the smallest in the county, the surrounding areas had large population swells.

He wasn't choosing women based on appearance, career, or social status. What was he basing it on?

Samantha paused and rubbed her eyes, already weary. But she didn't have time to be tired. There was a life on the line. If she could do anything to help . . .

"Can't sleep either?" Elise shuffled into the kitchen, sporting bedhead and fuzzy Hello Kitty pajamas.

Samantha shook her head. "No, I had nightmares. Kept hearing things."

"No updates?"

Samantha shrugged. "If there are, no one has told me. I'm sure I'm not first on their list."

"I still can't believe this has started up again." Her voice sounded as somber as Samantha felt. Elise lowered herself into the chair beside her.

"This man has already taken away so much of my

life, and now he's returned to take even more." That had been her resounding thought last night.

He couldn't wreck her life again. Yet it was like she could see an accident about to happen, and her entire body was bracing herself for the incoming impact.

Elise frowned and poured herself some coffee. "Maybe the police will catch him this time."

"We can only hope."

Silence stretched between them, and Samantha took another sip of her coffee. She'd been obsessed lately with Almond Joy-flavored creamer. Elise had introduced her to the variety. But nothing really tasted good right now.

"Who was that FBI agent who came in with you last night?" Elise asked, shifting in her chair.

Quinn's face fluttered through Samantha's mind, especially his kind eyes. Why couldn't every agent be like him? Maybe she wouldn't have so many knots in her stomach if they were.

"They call him Quinn," she said.

"Nice guy?"

"Yes, he is. One hundred times better than Frost."

"Frost is terrible. Maybe you can report him. He doesn't need to work with the public. That's for sure."

Elise had heard about Samantha's encounters

with Frost before. He'd been a topic of many conversations. "I don't want to waste my energy on him. He's not worth it."

"Good point. But he has a major attitude problem."

"Agreed." But Samantha had suspicions that it was more than his attitude that was a problem. Through a twist of fate, she knew too much about the man. She'd learned his deepest, darkest secret. Around that same time, Frost had begun to act resentful of her.

"Now, Quinn on the other hand . . ." Elise raised her eyebrows.

She studied her friend, curious now about what she was hinting at. "Quinn what?"

"Quinn is very nice to look at." A smile curled her lip.

Samantha shrugged. She didn't want to admit that she'd noticed, but she had. "It doesn't matter. There are professional boundaries in place."

"Not for me." Her friend wagged her eyebrows.

Samantha laughed but inwardly felt a touch territorial. Which was ridiculous. She was perfectly content being single. And she in no way had her sights set on Quinn. She had far more important things to think about.

Just then, someone knocked at the door.

Samantha drew in a sharp breath and braced herself for whoever might be on the other side.

Quinn's stomach churned as he stood outside Elise's house and prepared himself to update Samantha. He had no doubt that this would be an impossibly hard day for her, and he wished he could change that. But he couldn't.

He tugged up the collar on his thick black parka and wished he had more coffee. He'd worked all night, only pausing long enough to take a shower before coming here. There was no time for sleep right now.

Samantha cracked the door open, only one eye showing and the chain still attached.

She was being cautious; that was good. But anyone skilled could easily push past such a flimsy chain and get into the house. He didn't like that thought.

When Samantha saw him, she opened the door fully, and pushed her thick hair back. Her eyes looked uncertain again—partly intrepid, partly curious. Altogether lovely still.

"I didn't expect you to come by," she said.

Another cold wind brushed over him, reminding

him of the brutality of the task at hand. "Can I come in?"

She nodded and stepped aside. He waved hello to Elise when she peered around the corner from the kitchen, not feeling quite presentable yet, if he had to guess.

"What brings you by?" Samantha's voice sounded strained as she crossed her arms, pulling her dark blue sweater closer.

"A couple of things."

She nodded toward the kitchen. "How about if I get you some coffee? You look tired."

"Coffee sounds great." He followed her into the kitchen. Her friend must have slipped around the corner and out of sight because it was just the two of them.

Samantha poured him a cup, set it in front of him with the fixings, and lowered herself across from him. "So what's going on?"

He took a sip of his coffee—he liked his black—and then leaned back. The weight of this and how it would affect Samantha's life wasn't lost on him. "Well, we've been exploring several theories. The first person we looked at was Mandy's ex-husband. We wondered if he was acting as a copycat to throw the police off."

"A copycat? Really?" Surprise etched her features.

"It was just a theory. If her ex knew anything about the Grim Wrecker, then he could have followed the details that were written in various news articles. It would be the perfect cover for doing away with his wife. He wouldn't have to pay alimony. He'd been a lawyer. A very expensive lawyer."

"But the MO matches the Grim Wrecker to a T. And there was that letter. And then there was that phone call to me."

"It's true. But it's still a theory we're playing with."

Samantha studied his face for a moment, her fingers gripping her coffee mug. "There's more."

He nodded solemnly before starting. She was observant. That was a good thing. "Someone called in a lead this morning. He didn't leave his name, but he directed us to an old hunting cabin. He claimed he came across it a couple of months ago, and that it could match the description of where the women were held."

"And?" She rubbed her throat.

"And it appears that this could be the killer's lair, so to speak. We're investigating it now, but any DNA samples we find there will take a while to come back."

She dropped her gaze but only for a minute. She

pulled it back up with a new hope in her eyes. "Was Mandy there?"

Quinn shook his head, hating that he didn't have better news. "No, it was empty. It didn't look like it had been touched for a while."

"I see." Disappointment tinged her voice.

He took another sip of coffee, trying not to rush the conversation. "We're hoping you might come down there and see if anything is familiar to you."

Her face paled.

Quinn waited for her to process everything. In his gut, he knew what her decision would be.

Finally, Samantha nodded. "I'll go. Maybe something will ring a bell."

"I know this has to be incredibly difficult for you. All of it. But if this is the right place . . ."

She nudged her chin higher. "I can do it. Especially if it might help someone else. Let me finish getting ready first."

CHAPTER 10

SAMANTHA WASN'T sure she was ready to see this cabin. Her throat kept constricting until she felt as if she couldn't breathe. Her heart hammered out of control. Her palms felt sweaty.

Yet she knew she had to do this. The implications of finding this cabin were bigger than her and anything she might be feeling. It could save lives.

She stared out the window of Quinn's sedan at what looked like a premature winter landscape. More snow had come down last night, not enough to cover the ground, but enough to leave patches in crevices and shady areas. Those expanses matched the chill she felt in her soul.

By the time they drove down the winding mountain roads and onto a gravel road and then onto a dirt road, Samantha's limbs were a trembling mess. As hard as she willed herself to quit shaking, she couldn't stop.

They pulled to a spot at the end of a long, wooded drive. It was secluded here, and the driveway was hardly visible unless you were looking for it. Obviously, other law enforcement had been doing just that because there were probably eight other vehicles here already.

The cabin in front of her was small and old and unkempt. Weeds grew up around the sides. One window had plywood over it—old plywood that was falling off. Rickety-looking wooden steps led to a small wooden porch.

A screen door feebly guarded the bland brown door behind it. Samantha closed her eyes, remembering the sounds of the man approaching. The crunch of his tires against gravel. His heavy footsteps on a wooden porch. The sound of a door opening. Or had there been two doors?

She pressed her eyelids together harder as the memories transported her back in time.

What were those noises?

At once, they hit her again. A screeching sound, followed by a whoosh of air.

Yes, Samantha decided. There were two doors. A squeaky screen door and a heavy wooden one.

Her tremble deepened as the memories—at one time vague—suddenly seemed more real than ever.

Agent Quinn didn't open his door, even after he put the car in Park. He sat there, the seconds ticking between them. Icy flakes hit the windshield. Branches clattered together. Leaves scurried away with the wind.

It was like nature knew the horrors that may have happened here and mourned with them.

"I wish there was something I could do to make this easier." Quinn's low voice helped calm her nerves.

"I appreciate that. But I just need to get this over with." Even as she said the words, she made no attempt to move. Nor did Quinn pressure her.

Finally, after taking several calming breaths, she nodded. "Let's go."

They stepped from the car, and Quinn remained at Samantha's side as they walked toward the cabin —toward her nightmare. Her place of terror. Maybe. If this was the right location.

Quinn cupped her elbow as they walked up the stairs. He feared she would pass out again, she realized. And she might.

Samantha recognized that, visually, none of this would matter. It was her other senses that would take her back in time. The smells. The sounds. The feel.

She wanted this to be the place yet didn't want it to be. She needed answers. Law enforcement needed answers. The families of the victims deserved more closure.

But she wasn't convinced she could face this.

As they stepped inside, Samantha froze in the entryway.

The place was ramshackle, which fit her recollections. She remembered feeling the grit against her shoes. Remembered smelling decay. Remembered the rough tweed of the old couch beneath her.

It was small inside. A tiny kitchen took up residence in the far left corner. The sink there overflowed with dirty dishes that looked years old. Roaches scurried across the yellowed plates. Sauce was splattered on the stove and counter.

At least Samantha hoped it was sauce.

Her stomach revolted at the thought.

There was also a small table in the corner. Junk was piled high on it. There were old coffee cans, fishing hooks, plates, and pre-packaged food wrappers.

A pea-green tweed couch sat on the opposite wall with an old woven rug in front of it.

Could that be the couch where she'd been prisoner? The dirty rug she'd felt beneath her stockinged feet?

Quinn's grip on her elbow tightened, but he said nothing. He was giving her space to process, and she deeply appreciated that.

There was no need to go any farther in the house. To her knowledge, this was as far as she'd gone. That couch had been her dungeon for three days—if it was the right one.

"Anything?" Quinn finally asked, his voice full of compassion.

"I'm not sure." Remembering grit on her feet didn't quite seem like enough to verify this was the place. She couldn't haphazardly give an answer, either. Too much was on the line.

"Take as much time as you need."

Samantha took another step forward and closed her eyes. There was too much noise around for her to remember the sounds of the house. The door was open and a frigid wind swept inside, extinguishing any familiar scents as well.

She needed something else to jog her memory.

"Could I sit on the couch?" Her throat felt achy as the words left her lips.

Quinn glanced at someone—probably a CSI—who gave him a nod.

Slowly, Samantha lowered herself on a filthy cushion. Her hands brushed the fabric and sent another round of nausea through her.

It felt the same as the one from her nightmares.

The dust that rose from the cushions held familiar scents of age and woods and neglect. But she needed more.

"Is there a frame beneath this?" she asked.

"A frame?" Quinn repeated, his warm brown eyes accessing her.

She nodded. "I was tied to something. I assume the rope was attached to a sofa bed maybe. Possibly the sofa frame. I'm not sure."

He motioned for his guys to check. She stood and watched with bated breath as they took the cushions off. Sure enough, there was a hidden bed there. And on one of the metal frames were wear marks, just as if a rope had rubbed against the metal and worn off the black paint.

Her nausea grew.

When she saw the fireplace across from her, the truth crept closer and closer.

That was the fireplace that had crackled as though the gates of hell had opened and were taunting her.

She took three steps toward it. Heard a creak. The creak.

The one that she'd always heard as the man approached her.

This was the place, she realized with certainty.

Everything went white around her.

CHAPTER 11

AT ONCE, Samantha was back in the watery depths of that partially frozen pond from her nightmares. That familiar layer of clear ice was there, separating her from the help just on the other side.

As always, she was unable to scream. Unable to get any attention.

Her fist banged against the ice, hoping to break it. But it was too thick.

She couldn't breathe. Water began filling her lungs, drowning her. Hypothermia stole the feeling in her extremities.

And it would be so easy to close her eyes and just let go of everything. To let go of life.

But Samantha couldn't allow herself to do that.

No, she wasn't beneath the surface, she realized.

But the memory was—the one that begged for her attention.

Whatever her memory was, it lingered at the surface. It was so close yet just out of reach. If she could just break through and retrieve it . . . instead, she disappeared into the pond with it.

"Samantha? Samantha?"

Her thoughts tried to come back to the present. Tried to be rescued from her icy grave.

But part of her didn't want to.

Maybe she could stay here. Conscious yet unconscious. Part of her didn't want to face reality. Being in this state of oblivion was a welcome break from the painful memories.

The truth was there. If she could just survive down here another moment. Maybe then the answers would become clearer.

But someone shook her again, rumbling the water around her. She couldn't fight the pressure to emerge anymore. She pulled her eyes open.

She'd passed out. Again.

Maybe these memories were too much for her to handle. Maybe her body shut down in order to cope.

As she blinked, Agent Quinn's face came into view. They were in a bleak room. Cold air surrounded them.

Frost peered at her, as well as two officers.

Quinn's arm slipped around her back, and he helped her to sit up there on the dirty floor.

When she realized where she was, nausea pooled in her gut again. The grit beneath her. The squeaky floor underfoot. That horrid couch.

"This was too much for you," Quinn said.

Samantha shook her head, hating the fact she was making a spectacle of herself. Wishing she was stronger and more capable and more in control. But she wasn't. She'd thought she was at one time, but tragedy had humbled her. Sweat covered her palms.

"This . . . this is the place," she muttered, the life draining from her as the words left her lips. She held onto Quinn, afraid she'd hit the floor again.

Frost's phone rang and he stepped away. Even having the man farther away made her feel better.

"Are you sure this is the place?" Quinn asked.

She nodded, but the motion caused everything to swirl around her, made her feel like she was inside a snow globe that a toddler was shaking. "Yeah, I'm sure."

Frost put away his phone and approached them again. "I just heard back about who owns this place."

"Who?" Quinn asked.

"Aaron Jeffries."

The blood drained from Samantha's face. Aaron?

Her old high school classmate and the friendly town paramedic?

Could he have really been behind all this?

She didn't want to believe it. But she'd always suspected the Grim Wrecker was someone she knew.

CHAPTER 12

QUINN LEFT Samantha in the car as he and six other law enforcement officers surrounded the fire station where Aaron Jefferies was working. He'd go in to talk to Aaron—calmly, he hoped. But he needed the men outside as backup, just in case the guy decided to run or do something else foolish.

He didn't feel comfortable leaving Samantha alone right now—not until they knew for sure where Aaron was and until they confirmed he was their guy. Instead, he directed a sheriff's deputy to stay with her, just to be safe. He couldn't take any chances.

Aaron fit the profile on so many different levels. He knew Samantha. He knew the area. He would have been in the middle of the action when the bodies were discovered. For a serial killer, that could be just the buzz he needed.

Could the Grim Wrecker have been under their nose this whole time and no one had seen it?

When the building was sufficiently surrounded—and there was nowhere for Aaron to run—Quinn and Frost entered the station. The fire chief—whom Quinn had already spoken with on the way here—greeted them somberly at the front and directed them to a space toward the back.

They walked into a break room and saw Aaron sitting there eating a sandwich and reading the newspaper. He straightened when he saw them, visibly tensing.

"You guys are with the FBI," he muttered, setting his sandwich down. "What's going on?"

"We have some questions for you, Aaron," Frost said.

His eyes widened with confusion. "For me? Sure. What do you need?"

"We know about your cabin," Quinn said.

The confusion remained in his eyes. "What cabin?"

Quinn wasn't sure if he was playing dumb or not, but he couldn't let this guy off the hook yet. He was their best lead. "The one down in Miller's Hollow."

Aaron's shoulders slumped slightly. "My granddad's old place? I haven't been there in years. What's going on? What's the big deal about the cabin?"

Frost crossed his arms and glowered at Aaron. "When was the last time you were there?"

"I don't understand . . ." He braced his palms on the table top.

"Just answer the question," Quinn said. "When was the last time you were there?"

He shrugged, his surprise morphing into the beginnings of panic. "Probably when I was fifteen. Before my granddad passed. I used to go there with him on fishing trips. Now that I think about it, some guys from high school and I took a trip there after I graduated. That was the last time I went. Now, what's going on?"

Frost continued to stare at him, his eyes intense. "When did you take ownership?"

"My granddad passed away five years ago. I haven't had the heart to sell it. I'm not a hunter or fisherman myself."

The man seemed to be telling the truth, but Quinn would take nothing for granted. Thoroughness was an asset right now. "Where were you yesterday?"

"You saw me." His voice rose in pitch as his nerves obviously began to get the best of him as a sheen covered his skin. "I was at the scene of the crime. I helped Samantha after she passed out."

Frost leaned closer, going full-on with his bad cop persona. Or maybe it wasn't a persona. "Did you come back to gloat? Because you get some kind of sick high out of seeing officers on the scene? Maybe you called Samantha just so you could see her reaction when she realized who she was speaking with."

Aaron's eyes widened.

"Wait. You think I'm the Grim Wrecker?" His voice pitched upward.

Frost continued to stare. "You know a thing or two about cars, don't you? You could easily sabotage them."

"So do most of the men in this area. That doesn't mean we're all killers."

"We strongly suspect that cabin is where all the victims have been kept," Quinn said. "It's your cabin."

Aaron stood and raised his hands, his face deathly pale. "Then I'm being framed. I would never do this. You've got to know that. I'm in the business of helping people. That's why I became a paramedic."

"Could you come down to the station so we could talk then?" Quinn said.

Aaron looked left and then right.

And then he darted toward the door behind him.

❄

Samantha watched as the officers outside the building took off in a run. Her breath caught. What was going on?

At once she saw Aaron.

He was running. Why would he do that?

Unless he was guilty.

Her heart pounded furiously. She didn't want to believe he could be behind this. He'd always been nothing but kind to her.

Elise's words came back to her. *He's always had a crush on you.*

That couldn't be true. The two of them had always just been friends.

The man didn't have a chance to escape, not with so many officers. Two of them easily tackled him. A moment later, Quinn and Frost appeared and hand-cuffed him.

Aaron was placed in a police cruiser before Quinn climbed back in the car with her.

"Is he the Grim Wrecker?" Her voice cracking with every other word.

"It's his grandfather's old cabin. He claims he hasn't been there in years. Can you think of any connection he may have had to any of the victims?"

"We went to high school with one. It's a small

town. I'm sure he knew the others. Maybe he responded to emergency calls at their houses?"

"It's a theory worth looking into."

Back at the sheriff's office, Samantha was quarantined in the lounge area. Until Quinn knew for sure that Aaron was behind this, she had to stay. Or, at least, they strongly recommended for her own safety and well-being that she not go anywhere else.

While sitting on a leather couch, an icy knot in her stomach, Samantha kept replaying the events from yesterday. Some detail begged for her attention. Something that didn't make sense.

If Aaron had been the one who called her yesterday while at Mandy's car, Samantha would have heard more than silence in the background. Officers were talking all around her during that call. Another police cruiser had pulled up, lights and sirens blazing.

It had been too quiet on the other end of that phone line.

Her gut told her that Aaron wasn't the person who'd done this.

Yet he'd owned that cabin.

Was that a coincidence? Or had he been set up?

The waiting was killing her.

Someone brought her a sandwich. She forced

herself to eat. The ham and cheese had been tasteless to her.

Her attention was drawn to a flurry of activity in the conference room, and her spine tightened.

Something had happened. Something new.

She walked to the door, watching carefully. Holding her breath with anticipation.

Quinn's eyes met hers through the glass, and she saw the grief there. She knew something was wrong.

He walked toward the door and slipped into the hallway.

"What's going on?" she asked.

"Someone found Mandy," he said.

She froze. "And?"

"She's dead."

CHAPTER 13

I NEED MORE. I can't resist.

I fist my hands and think about my conquest. A surge of delight rushes through me until my toes tingle.

The hunger is back. The hunger for revenge. To make people learn their lessons. It feels so good, so right, so much like . . . my destiny.

I glance at my watch again. I have a break right now where I can slip away. I can do what I need. I can follow my hunger until I'm satisfied.

I know who I need right now. I know the next woman who will die at my hands.

And nothing will stop me.

I pause and ball my hands into fists again. Except maybe Samantha.

But she hasn't reached out to me.

Maybe she will run to me when her heart breaks. It would be so much sweeter than me forcing her to become mine. With Samantha, my life would be complete. All my hurts would disappear.

I want my life to be complete.

Until then, I need to make my mark. Tell my story.

All as a faceless legend who makes people fear. I climb into my car, ready to begin again.

They used to say I was a nobody.

But look at me now.

I was a headline maker, the one that every woman was talking about.

And there is still more to come.

I put my keys into my ignition and take off down the road, my next victim only minutes away from having her life turned upside down.

CHAPTER 14

QUINN WENT to check the scene where Mandy's body had been discovered. Whereas other women had been left in shallow graves at isolated, private cemeteries, Mandy had been left by a stream, not far from the roadside. Some fishermen had discovered her on one of the rocky boulders there.

Samantha didn't know for sure—she was only theorizing—but she wondered if Mandy had been left here so her body would be discovered more quickly. Everything seemed accelerated for this murder, happening at a much more rapid speed than with the earlier killings.

As Quinn talked with investigators, Samantha remained in the car. Numbness washed over her.

It was horrible enough that Mandy had been snatched. But she was dead. Already. The Grim

Wrecker usually waited three days. Why was he changing his MO?

Samantha could only hope that in his rush, he'd been careless. Maybe he'd made a mistake that would allow the FBI to catch him. It would be the only good that could come out of a situation like this.

After three hours at the scene, Quinn returned to the car and sat down.

He looked pale, like he needed to sleep and eat. No doubt he'd been going nonstop since this started. Yet strength still emanated from him, an underlying calmness in his soul.

He didn't need to say anything. She knew the truth; this was heartbreaking.

He dropped his head back and let out a breath before turning toward her. "Listen, you want to grab a bite to eat?"

"Now?"

"Don't worry—I'll still be in work mode. But I might think more clearly with some food in my stomach. Maybe you will too."

She nodded, realizing she could use some nourishment also. "Okay then."

"Anywhere around here to get a good hamburger?"

"I know just the place."

She didn't ask any questions as they drove. She

wasn't sure she wanted to know the details of the crime scene. If she wanted to know if Mandy had been tortured. If her body showed signs of trauma. If she'd suffered.

Finally, they stopped at the Burger Shack, sat at a corner table surrounded by windows that displayed the majestic mountains in the background, and their food was delivered.

Quinn studied her a minute. "How'd you get through it, Samantha? You seem so calm right now."

His question surprised her. She thought Quinn would jump right into questions about the case. Instead, he was asking about her.

She didn't have to think very hard about her answer. She dwelt daily on the one thing that had grounded her. "Really, I wouldn't have gotten through any of this without my faith."

"Your faith in what?" He took a bite of his burger.

"In God. He's helped me to see a perspective outside of this world around me. A higher vision, of sorts. I want to use my tragedy to help others."

He wiped his mouth. "I like that. And I understand. I'm not sure how people do my job without believing that life is bigger than what we see around us."

Samantha's heart warmed at his words. "You've

been really kind to me, Quinn. I appreciate your compassion."

"It's my job to get to know people."

For some strange reason, his words made her feel deflated. It was ridiculous. Samantha knew that. She knew Quinn was only doing his job. So why did her emotions take a nose dive when he confirmed that?

"I like learning how people think, what makes them tick, what's shaped them into the person they are today," he continued.

Samantha nodded, determined not to show her disappointment. "I get that."

His gaze connected with hers. "But I do think you're a remarkable person, Samantha. And I don't say that to just anyone."

Heat filled her cheeks. Good heat. Heat that made her feel alive and warm—two things she couldn't say she always felt. But it was all ridiculous. How could she even care about things like that when there was a killer out there?

"This is a good burger," Quinn told her before taking another bite.

"I told you it was."

He stared out the window a moment, not saying anything.

A storm brewed in her gut as she realized what she needed to say, as an idea pressed on her until she couldn't deny it anymore. Quinn might think she was crazy. She could be wrong, and this could be a wild goose chase.

But she had to say it. "I think I know the killer."

His gaze jerked to her and he lowered his burger. "Why do you say that, Samantha?"

"My gut."

"Talk to me."

She shrugged. "I don't know how to explain it. But it's the only thing that makes sense. There's nothing I could have said to this man while in captivity that would have changed his mind and caused him to release me. So I either reminded him of someone he cared about or he did care about me."

"It sounds plausible. Any guesses who it might be? Talk to me. Not as a cop. Just talk, like you're having dinner with a friend."

Her gut twisted with hesitation, and her hamburger didn't seem as tasty as it had only seconds ago. "And if I'm wrong?"

"You're just theorizing. There's no right or wrong when you're brainstorming. It's just ideas."

She drew in a few deep breaths, trying to temper her thoughts. "It's all I've been thinking about. The fact that I know him is the only thing that makes sense."

He leaned closer, pushing his food aside. "Let me

tell you this to start you off. Aaron has an alibi. It wasn't him. He's been working a twelve-hour shift, and several people have verified that he's been with them the whole time."

Samantha nodded somberly at the news. She hadn't wanted it to be Aaron. Yet she had. She just wanted this guy stopped. "Okay."

"Who else might have taken an unusual interest in you?"

Hank's image came to mind. She hesitated to say his name. But what if her hesitancy led to someone else dying? "I've always suspected my boss, Hank, might like me."

Guilt pounded at her as soon as the words left her lips.

"Tell me about him."

"That night I was abducted I ran into him at the pharmacy. He was three years ahead of me in high school, so I knew him, but not well."

"What did he talk to you about that night?"

"General chitchat. There was a lawsuit against his nonprofit after one of the women he'd treated ended up committing suicide. The law firm I had been working with was representing him, and he was concerned about potential legal action. I couldn't really talk to him about it, so I just listened."

"And then?"

"I was getting nervous because we talked longer than I thought, and it was getting dark outside."

"And your mom needed her inhaler, right?"

She nodded. "That's right. It wasn't an emergency, but I wanted to have an inhaler on hand. When she gets stressed, it affects her breathing. I didn't want to take any chances. But I'd promised her I'd be back before dark."

"Go on."

"Hank offered to give me a ride back, but I told him no. And then . . ." She didn't have to finish because Quinn knew. Then the Grim Wrecker had abducted her.

"Now you work for Hank?" Quinn asked.

"That's right. When I needed a change, he was the first person I thought about. He was—is—doing a good work."

"What's he like? Other than the fact he likes to help people."

She picked up a fry, thought about eating it, but then changed her mind and placed it back on her plate. "He's kind of shy, actually. A little quiet and awkward. He doesn't really care a lot about money. I'm pretty sure he doesn't even always get paid. It's all about fundraising and grants."

"He's single?"

"That's right. Never been married, to my knowledge."

She shifted as her thoughts went somewhere she hadn't wanted them to go.

"What is it?" Quinn asked.

"There's one other person who keeps popping into my mind."

"Who's that?"

Her eyes met his. "Frost."

Quinn stared at Samantha, unsure if he'd heard her correctly. "Frost? Agent Frost?"

She pressed her lips together and looked out the window again.

"I have a strong suspicion about why he doesn't like me," she started, her voice strained.

"Okay."

"There are privacy reasons I'm not supposed to bring this up . . ."

"If you need to say it, then you should. Any little detail could help us right now."

She swallowed hard and kept her gaze averted. "His wife came to the women's shelter. I helped her start a new life somewhere else."

Quinn's heart pounded in his ears at her announcement. "Is that right?"

"This is all against the privacy policies we have. But since there's a serial killer out there and since you're FBI, then . . . I can't keep it to myself anymore." Her eyes finally met his, and he saw the tug-of-war there.

"Does Frost know that you were involved?"

She shrugged. "I'm not sure. Frost lives about an hour and a half from here. His wife purposefully came to us because we were away from her hometown and his connections there. I suspect that Frost knows that I know."

"So that would explain some of his hostility toward you." His stomach churned at the thought.

"Yes, it would."

"As despicable as that is, it doesn't make him a serial killer."

A touch of confidence returned to her eyes. "I know. It does shows his propensity to violence. When the Grim Wrecker called me, I also noticed that Frost was on the phone in the distance. Maybe he somehow muffled the other sounds around him. I don't know."

He tried to recall that memory. "I believe I'd asked him to check out some things for me."

"That's also true. But he would be in the perfect position to misdirect the FBI."

He let out a breath as he let that sink in. "I don't want to believe that's true."

"It's just a theory. One that I'm sharing . . . like I'm talking to a friend." Her eyes pleaded with him to understand.

He leaned back and thought about it another minute. The profile he'd put together was that of a person who was rejected, awkward, but who blended in. Maybe they did have some personal connection to the town. They definitely had some kind of connection to Samantha.

Could Frost be their guy? It was a possibility he needed to keep in mind.

"Let's keep this between us," he said. "Until we know something for sure, we don't want to tip anyone off."

CHAPTER 15

As they left the restaurant, Samantha texted Elise and told her she was on her way home. Elise texted back that she'd just left work and should get there about the same time. Samantha looked forward to spending some time with her friend away from all this craziness.

"I know it's been a rough day," Quinn said.

"It has been. I'd hoped all of that . . . would be for a purpose. That it would do some good. Instead, nothing changed. He still killed her."

"We think he set up Aaron, knowing that he was going to dump the body during that time. He must have called in the clue so we would investigate Aaron."

"So he's not dumb. He'd be pretty calculated."

"He is."

"So what is he planning next?" Samantha stared out the window. She wasn't sure she wanted to know. She'd hoped this would all end quickly.

A few minutes of silence passed.

Finally, Samantha cleared her throat. "He broke his MO. I mean, it's only been a day and Mandy is already dead and her body has been discovered. That's never happened before."

"You're correct."

"What does that mean? Why is he mixing things up?"

"We're not sure. Maybe he feels more confident. It could be the opposite. Maybe he fears being caught, and he wants to get rid of victims quickly. "

"Why target Aaron?" she continued, questions colliding in her head.

"That's something else we don't know."

"There are too many uncertainties right now. I don't like this."

"I know. But we're working as hard as we can. We have some of the best people in the agency on it."

She glanced at him. "Why'd you come here?"

"What was that?" he asked.

"You said you were in Houston, and now you're out here in the mountains of Virginia. Why?"

He shrugged. "I wanted a change."

"Don't most agents want to work their way up to bigger cities instead of the opposite?"

"I'm from Pennsylvania, and I wanted to be closer to home. Closer to my younger brother."

She supposed that explanation made sense.

"Our parents were murdered in a home invasion when we were teenagers," he continued.

"I'm so sorry." But now it made sense why he seemed so compassionate. He understood, in his own way, what she was going through.

Before they had time to talk anymore, Samantha spotted a car on the side of the road.

Her stomach sank, and it felt like the life drained from her.

"Quinn, that's Elise's car."

CHAPTER 16

QUINN PULLED TO A STOP, told Samantha to stay put, and he carefully exited his vehicle. He drew his gun as he approached the car at the side of the road.

He expected the worst. But he desperately hoped he was wrong.

As he rounded the car, he glanced inside. It was empty. There on the front seat was a generic key.

His stomach sank. He grabbed his phone and called for backup. Samantha had only talked to her friend thirty minutes ago. If the Grim Wrecker had grabbed Elise, they couldn't be but so far away. All the roads leading this way needed to be barricaded. They had to catch him.

As soon as he hit End, Samantha climbed from the car. She froze. Her eyes met his.

The truth washed over her.

She let out a guttural scream and bent over, almost as if physical pain had incapacitated her.

Quinn reached her in six strides and put his hand on her shoulder.

"We're blocking the roads off," he said. "Help is on the way. The Grim Wrecker just did this. It's not too late to catch him."

"But you won't." Her voice broke, and her hand covered her mouth. "This guy always slips away. He's always one step ahead."

He wanted to deny it, but he couldn't. Instead, he said, "There's always hope."

"Oh, Elise." Samantha let out another sob.

The sound squeezed Quinn's heart, and he pulled her into a hug. He couldn't imagine what she was going through.

They had to put an end to this before anyone else died. Somehow. Some way.

Three hours later, Samantha was still at the scene on the side of the road as the police searched for answers to no avail.

She huddled in Quinn's car, absorbing the warmth flowing through the vents. Someone had brought her some coffee and had offered a blanket—as if she'd been a victim.

And her mind reeled as she pictured what Elise must be going through right now.

Samantha had read the police reports. She knew what the other victims had endured. Things that no one should have to go through. Burn marks. Puncture wounds. Dehydration.

Her friend didn't deserve this.

And it was Samantha's fault.

For some reason, the Grim Wrecker seemed to be focusing his energies around Samantha. It wasn't acceptable. Other people shouldn't suffer because of her.

She rested her head on her hands again, a pounding headache trying to paralyze her.

Please, Lord, stop this. I know You have the power to do it. One word from You, and this man's rampage would end.

Yet they lived in a fallen world, one where man had freewill to do what he wanted.

A world that her hope was never supposed to be in. The struggles they had here would one day be dim compared to what waited beyond.

She straightened and forced down another sip of coffee. She needed to stay alert. In the distance, she

CHRISTY BARRITT

could see the agents clustered together. As her gaze drifted to Quinn, her muscles softened.

The man had been nothing but kind. She wasn't sure if that was just part of his job or if he was sincere. She hoped he was sincere in his compassion. It was so hard to trust people sometimes, though.

Her phone buzzed.

Her heart lurched when she looked at the screen and saw an unknown number.

Could it be . . .?

She flung the door open and motioned to Quinn. He wasn't watching. She searched for Frost even, but he was on the edge of the woods, his phone to his ear. She was going to have to do this on her own.

With trembling hands, she hit Answer.

Heavy breathing hit her ears. It was him. The Grim Wrecker. Again.

She was sure of it.

She sank back into the seat, afraid she might pass out.

"Let her go," she said, her throat achy with each word. "Please. She's my best friend. She doesn't deserve this."

Just more breathing.

"I'll do anything to save my friend. Take me instead of her. We can trade."

Quinn slipped inside the car as her sentences

faded. His eyes widened with alarm, concern. But she wouldn't take the words back.

She was desperate. The Grim Wrecker hadn't killed her three years ago. Maybe if Samantha traded herself for Elise, they could both live today.

"Please. I mean it," she finished, looking away from Quinn.

Before she could say anything else, the line went dead.

And so did her hope of finding Elise.

CHAPTER 17

SAMANTHA STARED AT THE PHONE, feeling halfway numb inside. Had she blown her chance to save her friend? Should she have tried a different approach? The what-ifs ran through her mind until her head swirled.

"What were you thinking?" Quinn muttered. "You offered yourself for Elise?"

"I was thinking that I don't want my friend to suffer."

His gaze burned into hers. "This guy is crazy, Samantha. He might just take you up on your offer. He might put you through a living nightmare again."

She raised her chin, knowing how it might have looked foolish from the outside looking in. But she'd meant her words. "Good. I'd rather it be me than Elise."

Quinn's scowl deepened. "He may not be as gracious if he captures you again."

"Quinn—" She stopped herself. What was she going to say? She wasn't even sure. Instead, she squeezed her eyes shut. "I don't know. I just want this to end. I'm not sure which is worse—living or dying."

"Samantha . . ." He lowered his voice. "I know what you went through with him."

Her cheeks flushed. She rarely talked about it. Most of her friends—even Elise—didn't know all the details. But, of course, Quinn had access to her files. He knew nearly as much as she did about her ordeal.

Knew she'd been starved. Knew her wrists and ankles were raw from her bindings. Knew her face was bloody from trying to rub her mask off. Knew the psychological torture she'd endured.

A tear escaped down her cheek. Quinn touched her arm, and, in the next instant, she was in his arms again. His strong, capable arms. Strong enough to hold up Mount Everest.

"I know you're scared," he murmured. "We're doing everything we can."

But were they? Was she? There had to be something else she could do.

She straightened as an idea came to mind. "I want

to go back to the cabin where I was held. Just you and me."

He pulled back and squinted, doing that familiar examination of her face. "Why?"

"I want to remember. The answers are there. I just know it."

"Samantha . . ."

"Please."

Quinn stared at her another minute before nodding. "Okay. If you're sure you can handle it."

"I can." Then she shook her head and corrected herself. "I will."

Samantha's palms were sweaty when they pulled up to the cabin again. She'd been here before, so she'd already experienced the initial shock of seeing this place.

Yet it felt like she hadn't. Being here felt new—frighteningly so.

Quinn held her elbow as they climbed the steps. Her throat tightened as the screen door screeched. As the bland brown door whooshed. As she stepped into the house of horrors.

Quinn's hand remained on her arm, and she was thankful for it. She wasn't sure how her body would react to all this. Part of her wanted to flee, to forget the sucker punch this place gave her. But she couldn't.

She had to face her fears head-on.

With just her and Quinn here, she'd be able to experience the cabin as it was. Quiet. Still. Without the chatter and clatter of multiple officers and CSIs.

"You don't have to do this," Quinn muttered. "You have nothing to prove. Don't let Frost get to you."

"Yes, yes, I do have to do this."

He closed the door, shutting out the frigid wind. "What do you need?"

Samantha glanced around, feeling quivery throughout every muscle and bone. "I just need quiet."

"I can do that."

She stepped from Quinn's grip toward the couch.

What had her psychologist told her? That senses could take people back in time.

That was what she needed her senses to do now.

She lowered herself down on those cushions and slipped her arms behind her, just as they'd been when she was bound. As the fabric brushed her hands, nausea rose in her.

The image of being here, being captive, filled her memory in an instant. Just as quickly, familiar fear washed over her. Hope—light, joy, life—began to fade.

She closed her eyes until all was dark. Like she had that hood on—the one that made her feel as if she couldn't get a deep breath.

Then silence surrounded her. The nothingness of being in the middle of nowhere. Of being unable to see

Samantha didn't want to do it, but she lay down, just as she'd lain while she'd been held here. Her cheek brushed the knotted fabric. The familiar scent of mildew and body odor filled her nostrils.

Images slammed into her mind, transporting her back in time.

In an instant, the ties on her wrists were real. Her hunger was real. The fear was real. All her plans for the future were gone in an instant.

The Grim Wrecker had grabbed her, and she had no means of escape.

Her breath caught as she heard a footstep. On the porch.

He was back.

The Grim Wrecker had returned.

What would this visit hold? Did Samantha want to find out?

She knew the answer. No. Absolutely not. She'd rather die here alone than face him again.

The screen door screamed. The front door opened.

He was here.

In the room.

With her.

She could hardly breathe.

Then another familiar feeling came over her again.

The trapped-under-the-ice feeling.

She was getting closer to the memory that had remained frozen beneath the surface. The ice was thinning, breaking, shattering.

A new sound found her. What was that noise?

It was unlike the other sounds.

It was a phone, she realized.

Her abductor had a phone with him?

She'd never remembered that before.

What would he do? Answer it? Let it go to voicemail?

Who was calling him? An accomplice? Someone who had no idea who he really was?

Samantha held her breath as she waited.

"Hello?" the man muttered.

Blood pounded in her ears, and she willed it to hush.

Why hadn't she ever remembered this phone call before?

"That's right. Okay. I understand that." His voice was dark and low. Maybe familiar, yet different. There was nothing especially distinct about it.

Who was he talking to? He almost sounded professional.

"What can I say?" he continued, lingering in the distance. "Bob's your uncle."

Bob's your uncle?

That phrase . . . where had Samantha heard it before?

The next instant, the man was standing above her.

"Sorry, Samantha," he muttered. "I'm so sorry."

Then electricity rocked her body.

He'd tased her, she realized.

And everything went black.

CHAPTER 18

THE MEMORY CAME BACK AGAIN. Samantha was in the partially frozen water. The ice was there. She could see things taking place around her. But it was blurry. And just far enough away from reality to make her desperate.

But help was there.

Bob's Your Uncle.

It was such a strange expression. Maybe it wasn't uncommon in some circles, but it was in hers.

Someone she knew used that expression. But who? Who was it?

The memories clawed at her. The surface of the ice continued to crack.

Something in her gut kept taking her back in time to high school. To that reunion she'd attended not long ago. To all the various faces she'd interacted with while she was there.

"Samantha?" Someone shook her.

Finally, she broke through the ice barrier. Reaching the surface. Desperately swallowing in gulps of air.

She pulled her eyes open with a start and sat up. Sweat covered her. Her heart raced.

And Quinn peered at her.

She was lying on that couch that she'd thought would be her coffin.

"Are you okay?" Quinn asked. "You were crying."

"Quinn, I need to go to Eastside High School," she told him.

"Why?"

"Because . . . I need to see the yearbook from the year I graduated. I don't know where mine is, and I . . . I remembered something."

"Talk to me, Samantha." He knelt beside her.

She swallowed hard, pushing herself up. She felt like she'd been hit by a truck. "Someone I went to school with used to say 'Bob's your uncle.' It means voilà, I think. I'm having trouble remembering who. But I think it may have been his yearbook quote."

"We can go to the school. Let me call Frost and tell him to meet us there."

Less than two minutes later, they were in his car, and Quinn turned on his siren as they sped toward town.

Neither said anything. And, as always, Samantha appreciated that fact again. Silence could be her healing.

They arrived at the school. It was a Saturday, so the students should be gone. There were some cars here, though. Maybe administrators or some football players going through extra practices. Probably the marching band as well.

There were also other FBI vehicles already here.

They went into the library. Agents were already pouring over the books. Samantha made her way past them and looked at those familiar yearbook pages. They seemed to sense her need and parted.

Everything seemed like gel around her as she flipped the pages.

Finally, she stopped at one picture.

The contents of her stomach threatened to rise.

The picture that stared back at her, with the quote beneath, was . . . Jed Hedges.

The high school nerd that Samantha had continually defended.

Her head swirled.

"That's the guy?" Quinn asked. "You're sure?"

Samantha nodded and pressed her hands into the

table. "He said that exact phrase. The memory was there beneath the surface the whole time." She grabbed her temple, a new pounding starting. "I just couldn't pull it out until now. Until my senses took me back in time."

"Frost, we've got to find out where Jed is now."

"I'll get right on that." Frost rushed from the room.

"Marks. Backer. You guys go too. We're going to need all the man power we can get on this case."

Samantha's head continued to pound, even when it was just her and Quinn.

Jed? Could he really be behind this? In her mind, she already knew the answer.

Yes, he could.

"You did a good job, Samantha."

"Thank you. But there's something else." She shook her head, trying to shake the memory free. "Quinn, I think Jed's family had a cabin down in Wallace Hollow. He talked about it sometimes when we were in band. It was . . . it was his happy place, if that makes sense."

"Wallace Hollow?"

"I'm pretty sure that's the place. I think it was someone who was like a grandma to him, but not directly related. The location may not show up in any searches."

"Let me call them." He pulled out his phone and stared at the screen. "I don't have service in here."

"Parts of the school are dead zones when it comes to cell service. It's been that way for as long as I can remember."

"Let me run down to the office then."

"I'll stay here. I could use a moment to collect my thoughts."

"If you're sure. I'll station an officer outside the door, just as a precaution."

"Got it."

When Quinn was gone, she hung her head. Would they find Elise in time? She prayed they would.

Suddenly, her nerves stood on edge. She needed to get out of here. She stood and walked toward the door. She'd promised Quinn she'd stay here, but she'd feel better if she found everyone. She didn't want to be alone right now.

As she reached the door, she saw that a chain had been locked over the two metal handles.

What? That couldn't be right?

Someone would have to place them there from the inside.

And there was no one in this room with her.

Right?

She turned around to double check when an electrical shock rushed through her body.

She fell to the ground.

When her vision cleared, she could barely make out Jed's face above her.

CHAPTER 19

"You'll never believe this," Frost muttered, staring at his computer he'd set up in the school's office.

Quinn went to stand behind him, curious about what he'd learned. "What's that?"

"This Jed guy? He just got a job."

Quinn narrowed his eyes, wondering where he was going with this. "Doing what?"

Frost pulled his gaze up to meet his. "Working as a custodian here at the school."

Quinn's heart rate ratcheted up to the sky. Was he here now?

He wasn't going to wait around to find out.

He sprinted down the hall and reached the library. The guard he'd stationed outside was on the floor. He put a hand to his neck. There was still a pulse there. He radioed for help before tugging the door. It was locked.

Locked?

He glanced through the glass and saw the chain there.

His stomach sank.

Jed had been here, he realized.

He rattled the doors again. There had to be another way to get in.

Jed couldn't be but so far away. Where had he taken Samantha?

He pulled out his gun and shot out the glass window atop the door.

Footsteps sounded behind him as other agents hurried his way.

He climbed through the broken glass and rushed toward the desk where he'd left Samantha.

There on top of the yearbook was a key.

"Split up!" he yelled. "We've got to find her. Now."

Samantha sensed Jed pulling her into a room beside the library. They wouldn't make it out of the building without being spotted . . . right? He was keeping her at the school somewhere.

The resource closet, she realized. It was where all the equipment was kept. Projectors and other electronics. Only one door in.

She glanced up.

But there was a glass frame on the door.

If only she could move. If she could scream. If she could let someone know she was here.

"I'm sorry, Samantha," Jed muttered, sweat pouring off his forehead. "I didn't want it to happen this way."

It doesn't have to! She wanted to scream.

But she couldn't. She couldn't say anything. Not until her shock wore off and her muscles returned to life.

Jed was just as tall and lanky as ever. His face was pale—almost gaunt. His dark-brown hair was cut in a bowl cut, but it was greasy. He wore a janitor's uniform.

Jed was wearing a janitor's uniform. Did he work here at the school? Now that she thought about it, it did sound familiar.

When had she seen Jed last?

That was when she remembered.

The high school reunion last month. It had been right here at the school.

Only Jed hadn't attended as a participant, had he? He'd been working the event. Standing in the background. Watching. She'd even gone over to talk to him that night, but he'd been strangely silent. She hadn't realized he was a janitor. She'd figured he was on the committee or something.

Another sound hit her ears. Someone was pounding at the doors.

Quinn! Had he come back? Had he realized the truth?

"You weren't supposed to come here today," Jed whispered, standing over her. "I was going to head back and take care of Elise. I'd probably call you again. I like hearing your voice."

Samantha tried to move her lips, but she couldn't.

"I didn't want to do this," Jed continued. "The reunion put me over the edge. It brought back so many memories. My mom died in that auto accident when I was only eleven. Do you remember that? She was the only one who protected me from my father. He was a horrid man. He died four years ago from a drug overdose. That's what the police think, at least."

Her stomach squeezed. Jed had been through a lot. But none of that excused what he'd done.

"Now I have to figure out what to do with you." He reached behind him and pulled out a gun. "Like any good killer, I have a backup plan."

A gun? That didn't fit. What would he do with that gun? Shoot her?

Just then, a loud bang filled the room.

She froze. Was that Jed? No, it had come from the library.

Quinn?

Samantha moved her lips again. This time, a sound emerged.

Her voice was coming back.

"Why, Jed?" she whispered, her voice hoarse. "Why are you doing this?"

He wiped his forehead. "Because people need to pay."

"To pay for what?" She tried to move her legs, but it felt like they were bound. She knew they weren't. The effects of the Taser were still wearing off.

"What they've done." He flung his gun in the air, talking with his hands.

"What have they done?" she continued, trying to buy time. She tried to move her legs again. Maybe the muscle control was coming back. Maybe.

"They've made me feel like less." He sneered and stared at that window.

"Talk to me. How have they made you feel that way?"

"They've rejected me."

"Even Mandy?" she asked.

There. Her leg moved.

She didn't want Jed to see it, though. Instead, her

gaze focused on the Taser he'd left on the carpet beside him. If only she could reach it.

Jed's gaze darkened. "Yes, even Mandy. I met her online. She seemed to like me. Then she met me in person. Realized I was a janitor. That I was awkward. She ended the date early."

"I'm sorry. Trying to find a match isn't easy. I'm still single also. The last date I went on the guy stared at his phone the whole time and acted like I wasn't there."

"Then he was a fool. I'd love going on a date with you."

"Did all those women reject you?" She tried to understand, to buy time.

"They did. Some of them wouldn't give me the time of day. Others went on one date and then scoffed at me. One of them laughed at me when she passed me on the street."

"And Elise?"

"I asked her out in high school. She told me I wasn't her type. Then I heard her turn around and mutter, 'Freak.' It was supposed to be her that night, you know. Not you. From a distance . . ."

"We look alike."

"And you were driving her car."

Quinn appeared at the door and pounded on the glass. When he did, Jed put the gun to her head.

"Do anything and she dies," he yelled.

Quinn raised his hands. "It doesn't have to end like this."

Samantha swallowed hard, keenly aware of that gun. "Why Aaron? You set him up."

Jed's gaze darkened. "He invited three guys at the lunch table to go on his guys' weekend fishing trip after graduation." He sneered. "I was sitting right there. He just looked at me and said, 'Sorry, man. No losers allowed.' He's just as bad as all those women."

"That was wrong of them. Please let me go, Jed. Please."

He pressed the gun harder. "You weren't supposed to come here today. I needed your help. I begged for it. But you weren't supposed to come here."

"It's not too late to make things right. You asked for my help. I'm trying to give that to you now."

"No one can help me."

"I used to think that also. That no one could help me after my . . . my ordeal. But that's not true. There's always a light in the distance. We just have to make the choice to walk toward it instead of toward the darkness."

Her gaze remained on the Taser that he'd left on the floor. If she could just get a little closer.

"I don't think I can do it," he said.

"Sure you can. I promise you."

"I can't!" His words were lit with anger.

Samantha raised a hand. "Okay, okay. There's no need to get hyper here."

"You're the only one who's ever been kind to me."

"I'm sorry, Jed. You deserve kindness. Everyone does."

"People are going to remember me one day." He hung his head.

"Yes, they are."

If she was going to act, she had to act now while he wasn't looking. She reached over and her fingers gripped the Taser.

"Jed?" She rubbed her lips together.

"Yes?"

"I'm helping you now."

"What do you mean?" A wrinkle formed between his eyes.

And before he could realize what was happening, she sent a jolt of electricity through him. As he writhed on the floor, she darted toward the door. Her fingers fumbled with the lock.

But she got it open.

She fell into Quinn's arms as men rushed past them.

Maybe this was all finally over.

"Are you okay?" Quinn asked.

She nodded, not sure she was okay. But she was alive, and that was enough right now.

"We found Elise," he said. "She was where you said. Good work."

Her shoulders sagged. Maybe she could finally relax. This was over. It was finally over.

EPILOGUE

ONE THOUSAND TWO hundred forty-three days after she'd been released, someone knocked at Samantha's door.

This time, she didn't feel fear.

No, she knew who was on the other side.

She pulled the door open and saw Quinn standing there, that handsome grin on his face. Quinn, the one who always made her feel safe and calm—two qualities she didn't take for granted.

He opened the screen door, stepped inside, and kissed her cheek. "You look beautiful."

"Thank you. Did you have a good trip?" He'd driven the three hours from DC to see her, as he did most weekends. It worked for them—for now, at least.

"It's always good when I know you're waiting for me at the end of it."

She smiled, thinking about the twisted, winding road that had led them here to this place. If Jed hadn't abducted her, she might not have ever met Quinn. It was a blessing in the middle of a nightmare.

"Okay, before we actually relax like a normal couple, I have a few updates."

"Sit down. Let's hear them."

They sat beside each other on the couch—probably closer than necessary. But Samantha wasn't complaining.

"So, Jed has pleaded guilty."

Her heart lurched. He'd done the right thing by doing so. He'd been writing her letters from jail, and Samantha had encouraged him to do just that.

"Good."

"He's a very disturbed individual."

"I know."

He shifted. "I also wanted to let you know that Frost has been relieved of duty."

Her heart quickened. "What do you mean?"

"I mean that his ex-wife came forward and reported the abuse. He's off duty while they're investigating, but I heard the evidence is pretty rock solid. I don't think he stands a chance."

"Good. He should have consequences for what he did to her. I saw the bruises and the broken bones myself."

He rubbed her jaw with his thumb. "I think you're a remarkable woman, Samantha. Have I told you that?"

She smiled under his touch, under his compliment. "It wasn't that long ago that I thought my life was crumpled in pieces, much like a car after an accident. But it's possible to overcome the most broken days of our lives."

"It is. You're living proof."

ALSO BY CHRISTY BARRITT:

Hidden Currents

You can take the detective out of the investigation, but you can't take the investigator out of the detective. A notorious gang puts a bounty on Detective Cady Matthews's head after she takes down their leader, leaving her no choice but to hide until she can testify at trial. But her temporary home across the country on a remote North Carolina island isn't as peaceful as she initially thinks. Living under the new identity of Cassidy Livingston, she struggles to keep her investigative skills tucked away, especially after a body washes ashore. When local police bungle the murder investigation, she can't resist stepping in. But Cassidy is supposed to be keeping a low profile. One wrong move could lead to both her discovery and her demise. Can she bring justice to the island . . . or will the hidden currents surrounding her pull her under for good?

Flood Watch

The tide is high, and so is the danger on Lantern Beach. Still in hiding after infiltrating a dangerous gang, Cassidy Livingston just has to make it a few more months before she can testify at trial and resume her old life. But trouble keeps finding her, and Cassidy is pulled into a local investigation after a man mysteriously disappears from the island she now calls home. A recurring nightmare from her time undercover only muddies things, as does a visit from the parents of her handsome ex-Navy SEAL neighbor. When a friend's life is threatened, Cassidy must make choices that put her on the verge of blowing her cover. With a flood watch on her emotions and her life in a tangle, will Cassidy find the truth? Or will her past finally drown her?

Storm Surge

A storm is brewing hundreds of miles away, but its effects are devastating even from afar. Laid-back, loose, and light: that's Cassidy Livingston's new motto. But when a makeshift boat with a bloody cloth inside washes ashore near her oceanfront home, her detective instincts shift into gear . . . again. Seeking clues isn't the only thing on her mind—romance is heating up with next-door neighbor and former Navy SEAL Ty Chambers as well. Her heart wants the love and stability she's longed for her entire life. But her hidden identity only leads to a tidal wave of turbulence. As more answers emerge about the boat, the danger around her rises, creating a treacherous swell that threatens to reveal her past. Can Cassidy mind her own business, or will the storm surge of violence and corruption that has washed ashore on Lantern Beach leave her life in wreckage?

Dangerous Waters

Danger lurks on the horizon, leaving only two choices: find shelter or flee. Cassidy Livingston's new identity has begun to feel as comfortable as her favorite sweater. She's been tucked away on Lantern Beach for weeks, waiting to testify against a deadly gang, and is settling in to a new life she wants to last forever. When she thinks she spots someone malevolent from her past, panic swells inside her. If an enemy has found her, Cassidy won't be the only one who's a target. Everyone she's come to love will also be at risk. Dangerous waters threaten to pull her into an overpowering chasm she may never escape. Can Cassidy survive what lies ahead? Or has the tide fatally turned against her?

Perilous Riptide

Just when the current seems safer, an unseen danger emerges and threatens to destroy everything. When Cassidy Livingston finds a journal hidden deep in the recesses of her ice cream truck, her curiosity kicks into high gear. Islanders suspect that Elsa, the journal's owner, didn't die accidentally. Her final entry indicates their suspicions might be correct and that what Elsa observed on her final night may have led to her demise. Against the advice of Ty Chambers, her former Navy SEAL boyfriend, Cassidy taps into her detective skills and hunts for answers. But her search only leads to a skeletal body and trouble for both of them. As helplessness threatens to drown her, Cassidy is desperate to turn back time. Can Cassidy find what she needs to navigate the perilous situation? Or will the riptide surrounding her threaten everyone and everything Cassidy loves?

Deadly Undertow

The current's fatal pull is powerful, but so is one detective's will to live. When someone from Cassidy Livingston's past shows up on Lantern Beach and warns her of impending peril, opposing currents collide, threatening to drag her under. Running would be easy. But leaving would break her heart.

Cassidy must decipher between the truth and lies, between reality and deception. Even more importantly, she must decide whom to trust and whom to fear. Her life depends on it. As danger rises and answers surface, everything Cassidy thought she knew is tested. In order to survive, Cassidy must take drastic measures and end the battle against the ruthless gang DH-7 once and for all. But if her final mission fails, the consequences will be as deadly as the raging undertow.

Lantern Beach Romantic Suspense

Tides of Deception

Change has come to Lantern Beach: a new police chief, a new season, and . . . a new romance? Austin Brooks has loved Skye Lavinia from the moment they met, but the walls she keeps around her seem impenetrable. Skye knows Austin is the best thing to ever happen to her. Yet she also knows that if he learns the truth about her past, he'd be a fool not to run. A chance encounter brings secrets bubbling to the surface, and danger soon follows. Are the life-threatening events plaguing them really accidents . . . or is someone trying to send a deadly message? With the tides on Lantern Beach come deception and lies. One question remains—who will be swept away as the water shifts? And will it bring the end for Austin and Skye, or merely the beginning?

Shadow of Intrigue

For her entire life, Lisa Garth has felt like a supporting character in the drama of life. The designation never bothered her—until now. Lantern Beach, where she's settled and runs a popular restaurant, has boarded up for the season. The slower pace leaves her with too much time alone. Braden Dillinger came to Lantern Beach to try to heal. The former Special Forces officer returned from battle with invisible scars and diminished hope. But his recovery is hampered by the fact that an unknown enemy is trying to kill him. From the moment Lisa and Braden meet, danger ignites around them, and both are drawn into a web of intrigue that turns their lives upside down. As shadows creep in, will Lisa and Braden be able to shine a light on the peril around them? Or will the encroaching darkness turn their worst nightmares into reality?

On her way to completing a degree in forensic science, Gabby St. Claire drops out of school and starts her own crime-scene cleaning business. When a routine cleaning job uncovers a murder weapon the police overlooked, she realizes that the wrong person is in jail. She also realizes that crime scene cleaning might be the perfect career for utilizing her investigative skills.

#1 Hazardous Duty
#2 Suspicious Minds
#2.5 It Came Upon a Midnight Crime (novella)
#3 Organized Grime
#4 Dirty Deeds
#5 The Scum of All Fears
#6 To Love, Honor and Perish

When Holly Anna Paladin is given a year to live, she embraces her final days doing what she loves most—random acts of kindness. But when one of her extreme good deeds goes horribly wrong, implicating Holly in a string of murders, Holly is suddenly in a different kind of fight for her life. She knows one thing for sure: she only has a short amount of time to make a difference. And if helping the people she cares about puts her in danger, it's a risk worth taking.

THE WORST DETECTIVE EVER:

I'm not really a private detective. I just play one on TV.

Joey Darling, better known to the world as Raven Remington, detective extraordinaire, is trying to separate herself from her invincible alter ego. She played the spunky character for five years on the hit TV show *Relentless*, which catapulted her to fame and into the role of Hollywood's sweetheart. When her marriage falls apart, her finances dwindle to nothing, and her father disappears, Joey finds herself on the Outer Banks of North Carolina, trying to piece together her life away from the limelight. But as people continually mistake her for the character she played on TV, she's tasked with solving real life crimes . . . even though she's terrible at it.

ABOUT THE AUTHOR

USA Today has called Christy Barritt's books "scary, funny, passionate, and quirky."

Christy writes both mystery and romantic suspense novels that are clean with underlying messages of faith. Her books have won the Daphne du Maurier Award for Excellence in Suspense and Mystery, have been twice nominated for the Romantic Times Reviewers' Choice Award, and have finaled for both a Carol Award and Foreword Magazine's Book of the Year.

She is married to her Prince Charming, a man who thinks she's hilarious—but only when she's not trying to be. Christy is a self-proclaimed klutz, an avid music lover who's known for spontaneously bursting into song, and a road trip aficionado.

When she's not working or spending time with her family, she enjoys singing, playing the guitar, and exploring small, unsuspecting towns where people have no idea how accident-prone she is.

Find Christy online at:
www.christybarritt.com
www.facebook.com/christybarritt
www.twitter.com/cbarritt

Sign up for Christy's newsletter to get information on all of her latest releases here: **www.christybarritt. com/newsletter-sign-up/**

If you enjoyed this book, please consider leaving a review.